Something Really Wild

The bushes opened into a little glade, heavily shadowed, with leaves of sunlight sprinkled over it. Ellen saw the cat Scab nestled at the foot of a great dark boulder, or maybe an old, smoothed tree stump. It was hard to tell in the half-light.

Ellen stepped foward. In the warm summer air and soft shadows, Scab curled peacefully. The glade was thick with tranquility. She could hear Scab purring, and another sound...like Scab's, but deeper. It was coming from the boulder: or was it a tree stump?

As she watched, the shape stirred gently, then it raised its head.

Ellen gave a little jump of surprise. The head was as big as her own and two yellow eyes burned out of it.

Titles by Colin Pearce

Something Really Wild
Something Really Terrible
Something Really Dangerous

The One Minute Dream

something really
WILD

COLIN PEARCE
Illustrated by Elsie Lennox

Lions
An Imprint of HarperCollins*Publishers*

To my wife, Jenni; a very unusual woman who
swapped security for adventure, wealth for poverty,
and sanity for a lunatic life with me. With my thanks
and my love for ever.

First published in Lions in 1991

Lions is an imprint of HarperCollins Children's Books,
a Division of HarperCollins Publishers Ltd,
77-85 Fulham Palace Road, Hammersmith, London W6 8JB

ISBN: 0 00 674278-5

Printed and bound in Great Britain by
HarperCollins Manufacturing Ltd, Glasgow

One

"Why couldn't we buy a new house; with a nice neat lawn?" called Emily, picking up a loose piece of crumbling brick out of the wall. "And walls that aren't falling down."

The grunting from the kitchen had stopped. That meant the fridge was in place.

"Because we couldn't afford it," she heard her father call. "And we wouldn't want one anyway. These victorian places will still be standing when those modern boxes have all . . ." more grunting, ". . . all fallen apart."

Emily dug at a windowsill with the piece of brick. The wood crumbled and fell away in soft, black flakes.

"But this one's falling to bits *now*!"

She stepped back suddenly as dust and debris fell in a cloud from an open window above onto her gingery hair. That's why it's cheap," said her mother's voice from the window.

Emily eyed the falling dust gloomily. "I liked the old place. At least it was tidy; well, tidy for us. And I had loads of friends. Now I've got to spend the summer holidays on my own, go to a new school where I don't know anyone and . . . and . . . tchoo!"

The dust clouded around Emily's head and she sneezed. ". . . and live in chaos again for years while you sort it out."

Her mother's head appeared at an upstairs window. She had a scarf tied over her hair; her nose was shiny with perspiration and grubby with dust.

She was like an older version of her daughter, with hair which she called red (but which was ginger) and the same slender figure.

"You could always help," called her mother grimly. "I've finished in the dining room; how about cleaning the windows?"

Emily stopped digging holes in the windowsill and tossed the brick away quickly, pointing to the rabbit hutch beside her. "I'm, er . . . I'm still feeding Sounds."

"Well, stop moaning and do it then." The head disappeared.

Emily strolled over to the edge of the paved area outside the house and tore up another handful of dandelion leaves. Her eyes met the wall of foliage and bramble towering before her like a green storm. She shook her head despairingly, calling back over her shoulder, sarcastically, "When are you going to do the garden; in your spare time?"

She heard a crash as something very breakable met with the kitchen floor and her father's voice bellowed: "For God's sake, Emily. Shove off and find something to do, or come and help. But don't stand there MOANING!"

6

Time to be somewhere else. She saw a small gap in the undergrowth. The brambles curled over, making a natural tunnel.

"*I* didn't drop anything," she muttered indignantly. Falling to her hands and knees, she crawled into the gap.

The tunnel ended where a thick, untamed shrub began. There was a little space beside it, in which Emily stood up. Behind her, through the thick, brambly undergrowth, she could see parts of the tall Victorian building which was now their home. It had been a grand house once, on the edge of town; but now the town was a city, and the estates had reached out and swallowed the original houses. Most of the big Victorian properties had been replaced by little orange-brick homes, like dice with roofs on. The huge gardens of the old properties had mostly been chopped up to make yet more estates.

But a few had escaped. Emily's new home and the houses on either side stood as a lonely, dilapidated group.

As the houses had fallen into decay so had the gardens. The grass grew scruffy and long-haired, blackberry bushes ran rampant across the lawns. Trees and shrubs dropped seeds at random, and the seeds grew randomly until they, too, were trees and shrubs; and the muddle grew forever outwards and upwards.

Emily chose a gap off to one side, still leading away from the house, and took it. She skirted around a little metal-framed rose arbour that was filled in with a tangle of thorny briar. She was no longer escaping; she was exploring.

She passed a garden shed. Ivy had forced its way between the weatherboard panels; through the dusty, cobwebbed window all she could see was ivy, looking back. A shrub had thrown a branch across the door, jamming it shut. It would wait; all around her the garden held promises.

A tingling excitement sneaked up her back. This was different; not just a mess. This was a personal kingdom; a private jungle; *her* private jungle. She imagined she might turn a corner and come face to face with some wild animal. With growing delight she pressed deeper into the undergrowth.

She came to a little clear patch where the grass was high and springy. A chestnut tree spread a light shade over the place; but still the warmth of the sun penetrated to the tall, wild grass. A movement in the branches caught her eye and she froze.

A cat was staring down at her through inscrutable green eyes; a cat that carried its character etched upon its face in battle scars. Half its left ear was missing, and the right was divided into three points where it had been shredded by claws. Across its nose Emily could see a deep groove disappearing into the fur. It was a tabby cat, whose barred coat was alternate shades of mud.

She held out a coaxing hand. The cat ignored it, remaining alert and tensed on its branch. Emily talked to it in a whisper, and the ears – the ear and a half – came forward, listening, while the eyes remained fixed upon her face. After a while the cat edged out of sight behind the tree trunk. A small sense of loss threw a shadow over Emily's thoughts, but she shrugged and walked on.

After a few steps the hair began to prickle on her neck. She sensed she was being watched. Turning, she saw the cat's ruined face staring fixedly back from the grass at the base of the tree. She made little kissing noises of encouragement through her pursed lips and it crept cautiously nearer.

It was enormous; powerfully muscled, more like a terrier than a cat. Even its tail was thick and short like a dog's, and it had a kink near the end where it had once been broken.

When it finally reached her she held out a hand. The cat froze, full of distrust. When nothing happened it pressed the side of its head hard against the hand – and purred; purring as big as the cat itself, rhythmic and intense, drowning out the sounds of birds and insects.

Emily smiled and whispered, "You're an ugly one, aren't you?" The cat ignored her, pushing and purring. "And big! The biggest cat I've ever seen."

A fly whined past and the cat batted it out of the air with casual but deadly accuracy, making Emily jump.

She laughed, "Where do you come from, you big brute?"

She wondered if he was a stray, and whether she dared take him home.

"No chance," she sighed to herself. "Not with

Mum's allergies. She'd go barmy." She stood up, reaching down with both hands as she did so, but the cat bobbed out from between them.

"Okay; follow me then. We can be friends, can't we? Come on . . . puss. Puss, puss."

She began the little coaxing noises again and strolled on, looking behind her. The cat came a short way after, and stopped. Emily moved behind a shrub, still calling, and waited.

"Puss, puss." She strained to hear the purring, but there was no sound. She hastily retraced her footsteps – nothing. The cat had vanished.

"Oh, don't go," she called plaintively. "Please! Puss, puss!" There was no sign of it. She snorted irritably and kicked at the grass. "Great ugly thing!" she pouted, more sorrowful than angry as she turned and walked away.

She had not gone far when she sensed, rather than heard, the merest thread of sound. She thought at first the cat had returned. She heard a faint squeak, and followed it.

The next sound froze Emily's footfall in mid-step. It was a giggle, a child's giggle.

Her breath was locked into her chest as the sound was joined by others, muted under the veil of the trees.

She took a step and gently eased a branch aside. Another voice sounded, quite clearly once the smothering effect of the shrubs was removed.

". . . won't bite. She'd probably be delighted."

Framed in the leaves was the speaker: a girl, older than Emily probably, but about the same height. It was hard to tell because she was sitting in a grassy clearing, her legs stretched out, arms behind propping her up. She wore a baggy T-shirt and fluorescent cycling shorts.

There was a boy with her, sitting tightly wrapped, his arms round his legs and his chin on his knees. He looked older than the girl. He was hollow-cheeked with hair shorn close around the sides and trimmed to a bristly flat-top. He spoke next.

"Well, *I'm* not going to do it."

A movement made Emily jump. Into view, so close she could have reached out and touched them, appeared two others. One – a boy – walked. The other – a girl – was dangling upside-down, her ankles locked in his hands. Her skirt was draped over her head, showing off her polka-dot pants.

After them trotted a dog; a tongue-lolling, rag-bag of a dog, the colour of rust, with hair in its eyes and a feathered tail which swept the air like a flag. The dog danced under the upside-down girl, trying to nuzzle her face under the cloak of the skirt. Her muffled giggle was the one Emily had heard earlier.

A small sense of indignation invaded her. This was *her* garden. She looked upon it as her personal discovery and she felt slightly irritated to find strangers using it as their own.

She took a deep breath and gave the branch a heavy shove. As it swept noisily aside she strode forward.

"Oh!" she gasped, feigning surprise.

11

The dog danced over and buried its nose in her hand, tail wagging. The dangling figure was lowered to the ground, where it quickly uncoiled to reveal a small girl, hardly even school age, round-faced and round-bodied, with solid arms and legs. Her shoulder-length hair was held in two high plaits.

"It's her!" she beamed, pointing to Emily. She turned to the others. "Well, *I* think she looks all right."

Her giggles spluttered against her hand.

The older girl jumped up. "Hmmpff," she snorted. "We should have let him drop you on your head."

She didn't smile but there was warmth in her wide, frank blue eyes. Her dark hair was swept back and tied carelessly with a bit of string.

She turned to Emily. "Don't listen to her. We get stuck with her in the holidays because her mum's at work all day. She's Ellen. Jamie's sister." She pointed to the hunched-up figure on the grass. "That's Jamie; he's the oldest. They live next door to you. Harry's my brother." She pointed to the smaller boy, whose eyes and mouth seemed to wear a permanent grin. He was younger; about Emily's age.

"We live the other side. I'm Lara," the girl said. "We saw you move in yesterday."

The small girl bounced over to Emily. She grinned through a fence of missing teeth.

"We were talking about you," she said. She pointed to each of the other children in turn, Lara first. "She gave you eight out of ten; Harry gave

12

you six out of ten . . ." In a loud whisper she added, "That's 'cos you're a girl."

She pointed to her brother, Jamie. "And he gave you—"

"Shut up Ellen!"

"—four out of ten." She shrieked and ducked behind Emily as Jamie hurled a stick.

Emily didn't know how to respond. She looked at Lara and gave a little shrug.

"She's showing off," Lara responded. "It's a drag, but . . . she's only five." She returned the shrug amicably.

The little girl was stroking the dog, which was still shoving its nose into Emily's hand.

"This is Feather," she said. "He won't hurt you. He's ours. Jamie's and mine. Well, Jamie's really. But Feather likes everyone, mostly. What's your name?"

"Emily. And . . ." she anticipated the next question as Ellen's mouth opened to ask it. ". . . I'm twelve. Well, nearly. In November."

"Same as me," said Harry as the dog tried to lick his face. He cuffed it idly. "Lara's thirteen."

"How did you know we were here?" he asked.

"I didn't. I was just exploring. I was looking for a cat. I thought maybe it came this way."

"What kind of ca—" Lara's question shut off abruptly, her gaze fixed on a spot beyond Emily. The others, too, were staring at a point behind Emily.

She followed their eyes. At the edge of the clearing a mud-grey battered face peered back.

13

Its eyes nailed Feather, but it took in everything around it with the tense caution of a veteran alley-cat. It padded forward to Emily's feet and wound itself between them. Emily could feel the purr resonating through her legs.

She was delighted. She reached down and scratched an ear. Feather took a step forward. The cat saw it and a growl – not a miaow or a hiss; but a real growl, like a dog – boiled out of its throat.

Feather put his tail down and trotted away behind Jamie.

Lara's mouth was open. "Not *that* cat?"

"How do you do that?" Harry asked Emily, his twinkling blue eyes wide with admiration.

"How do I do what?"

"Stroke it."

Emily was puzzled. "Why? Why shouldn't I?"

"No-one's ever been able to do it before. It's been around here for years. No-one owns it. Who'd want to! I mean, look at it. It's falling to bits."

Emily stared into the purring face and smiled. "He *is* a bit ugly, isn't he?"

"He attacked my mum once," said Ellen. "Scratched her right down her arm. It went septic and she had to go to hospital. It's vicious." She pointed to Feather. "He's terrified of it."

"Well, it seems to like me," Emily said earnestly. She bent down. She hadn't meant to pick it up, but somehow as she reached out the cat was already halfway into her arms. She folded it into her and stood upright again.

They were all dumbstruck. Lara spoke first. "Well! Worth at least ten out of ten. You must have some kind of gift."

Emily smiled with pride. "Maybe it just knows it's in my garden."

Jamie shook his head and spoke for the first time, blushing. "Not here, it's not. This is ours." He nodded towards a tree behind Emily. "That used to mark the boundary."

"Used to?"

Lara explained: "The fences fell down years ago, and no-one ever got round to putting them up again. They all talk about it – our parents, that is – but they're too busy."

Emily blushed. "Look, I'm sorry if I shouldn't be here. I didn't realize I'd wandered too far—"

Lara held up a hand. "No; we're glad. We'd much rather keep it as one big garden. It's been like this for years. It's really good for games. You're welcome." She pointed to the cat. "Especially if you can keep that thing under control." They grinned at each other.

"Has he got a name?" asked Ellen.

Emily shrugged. "We could give him one."

Lara said, "You're the one with the master touch; you choose."

Emily looked down at the cat, who watched her through slitted eyes. Emily was confronted with the deep scar across its nose.

"Scab," she decided.

"You can't call a cat Scab," cried Ellen, horrified.

Emily never got a chance to answer. There was

a crash as someone blundered through the under-growth, out of sight. It was followed by a coarse shout and a tearing noise; a branch being ripped from a tree.

A figure barged backwards into the clearing with a raucous laugh. Emily and the others watched silently. Scab wriggled free of Emily's hands; the purring had stopped.

It was a big, heavy-set boy, followed by two others, smaller. They all had stripped branches which they were wielding like swords.

They saw Emily and the others and stopped, their faces closing up, the eyes growing hard. The first boy appeared surprised for a moment before his face twisted into a leer. He swaggered forward, the branch swung casually over his shoulder.

His heavy jaw was balanced by a round, high forehead; his hair was cropped so close that it looked grey against his white scalp.

Emily could sense antipathy flowing from Lara and the others in the downturn of their mouths and the shielded nervousness in their eyes.

The bigger boy was standing directly in front of Jamie, looking down at him, threateningly close. "Wotcha, Jimmy-the-one," he crowed. He looked round at the others. "Baby sitting, are we?"

Jamie fiddled with a grass stem, not looking up.

"Haven't seen you since school," the boy went on. His gaze hardened as it swept over the others. "What's going on then?"

He stalked over to them, and stared at Emily.

16

He grinned again, but it wasn't friendly. "Who're you? New girl, are we? You playing Mummy, or Daddy?"

Emily sensed the situation would become openly hostile at the drop of a misplaced word. She looked at the others for help. Jamie stood and said: "Why don't you leave us alone?"

"Why should we? We haven't done any harm – yet."

Jamie pointed to the stick over the boy's shoulder. "You've torn down that," he said. "This is our garden and we didn't ask you into it."

"Garden!" jeered the boy. "You call this a garden! It's a slum, Jimmy-the-one. Tearing a few branches out is what it needs. Thinning, see? Pruning! . . . Anyway, what are you going to do about it?"

A low noise began that no-one could quite place; a faint rumbling sound. It took form and hardened.

Feather was growling. He stood beside Jamie with his head low and his eyes fixed on the other boy's face, the rumble from his throat deepening.

The set of the boy's shoulders slackened and the aggressive grin distorted into a scowl. He turned away, back to Emily.

"You must've moved in next door to this lot." He indicated the others with a sweep of his head. "Tough luck. You wanna get into something decent while you can. I'm Sean. Sean Beddock. This is Chrissie 'n' Mark."

He spotted Scab, standing stiff-legged at Emily's feet, and said: "You wanna watch out for that, too. It's always hanging around. Digging up the garden and messing everywhere. Not that it'd matter here, would it?" He roared at his own joke. Chrissie and Mark snickered obediently.

"My old man gave me an airgun. It don't come near our garden anymore. Just sting it a couple a' times and it stays away."

Emily was disgusted. She loved all animals, and her indignation lent her voice a courage she didn't feel. "If you were less like an animal he might treat you more like a human being," she said.

The others stared, open-mouthed. She knew she had gone too far, but there was no way of unsaying the words. Sean frowned, not sure whether the words had been as insulting as he imagined. His eyes alighted on the cat and he grinned nastily at Emily.

"This is how to handle him," he said, reaching down for the scruff of Scab's neck.

No-one really saw Scab move, but with a squeal of outrage and a blur of mud-brown fur he disengaged himself from Sean's hand and landed two metres away, kinked tail blown up like a bent bottlebrush. Sean dropped his branch and nursed his hand. Three score marks in the back of it were leaking blood down his extended fingers.

"Look what he did!" he gasped to Chrissie and Mark. He held his hand up to Jamie and the others. "Look what he did!"

Small, round Ellen stepped boldly forward against Lara's restraining hand. "Serves you right. You should try being nice sometimes, then people might be nice to you," she said.

18

She retreated again as she watched the menace smouldering in Sean's eyes. He, in turn, restrained himself under the threat of the long, low growl that once again issued from Feather's throat.

Behind the bigger boy Mark was uncertain how to react. He sniggered again, nudging Chrissie. Sean swivelled round and lunged out with a foot. "Shut it, you stupid . .!"

He left the sentence unfinished and strode off towards the edge of the clearing; Mark and Chrissie followed.

Sean turned. "You can't stay in here all summer," he snarled. "If I see any of you out on the street it'll be different. And if I ever get that cat I'll – I'll kill it."

He turned and strode off, shouldering the bushes apart. Mark and Chrissie followed him.

"Pheeeeew!" gasped Lara, throwing herself back on the grass. "Why doesn't he ever learn?"

Emily picked up Scab, whose tail was settling back to its normal size. "Who is he?" she asked.

Jamie said, "He lives at the other end of the road, where the new estate is." He squatted to fondle Feather as the dog sat looking up, tongue lolling, tail sweeping the grass.

"He's a bully, but it's worse at school when he's got all his mates with him. They're in the next year up from me. But mostly it's mouth. He'll forget about it."

He looked up at Emily. "It didn't help, you making smart remarks," he said curtly. She felt her cheeks flush hotly.

Jamie stood. "We've got to go. C'mon Ellen. Feather . . ."

The dog fell in beside him, but Ellen stayed where she was. "What for?" she said. "It's early. I want to stay here."

"Look, as far as I'm concerned you can stay here forever; but Mum said I had to get you back for lunch. So just do it and shut up."

She stamped off with Jamie and Feather loping behind. The remaining three sat in the soft grass and talked their way into the afternoon.

Two

There were seven forming the circle: the five children, Feather and Scab. The children were stretched on their stomachs in the clearing, looking

into the centre where Emily's rabbit, Sounds, sat systematically devouring dandelion leaves.

Scab was washing, but Feather was alert and restless; head up, eyes keen. Occasionally he whimpered and scrabbled at the grass. If Sounds stood, he stood, willing the rabbit to make a run for it.

Jamie put out a restraining hand and glanced scornfully at Emily. "Don't worry, he won't touch it."

"He might not eat it," said Emily. There was irritation in her voice. It seemed Jamie never spoke to her except harshly, and she was tired of it. "Maybe he'll just terrify the poor thing to death."

Harry was studying Sounds thoughtfully. "Doesn't he ever get tired of dandelions. We've done this every day for a week and he hasn't eaten anything else."

Emily nodded. "Gives him the runs. He's supposed to have oats and stuff, too. But I haven't got any money and Mum'n Dad say they can't afford it."

"If I had some money," said Lara, rolling on to her back and closing her eyes against the sunlight, "I'd get a horse. We could all take turns. Then at least we'd have something to do."

"You!" scoffed Harry. "As soon as you get your pocket money you're off buying those daft comics. You couldn't save enough for a sugar lump."

"Why don't we open a shop," said Ellen, kneeling. "A sweet shop with—"

"Shut up," said Jamie. "You don't know anything."

Emily stood, walked into the circle, and picked up Sounds. "The summer holidays are in the wrong place," she said. "I get loads of money at Christmas when you can't get out to do anything with it; but now the weather's great – and we're all broke."

Sounds ceased to represent an opportunity once he was in Emily's arms, and Feather lost interest. He wandered away to nose idly in the bushes.

"We could start a garden. Grow cabbages and things," volunteered Jamie.

Ellen pulled a face. "Yuk; it's bad enough having to eat it. I'm not growing it, too."

"Anyway, I like it here," said Emily. "What do we want to do anything else for? The garden's brilliant."

"You've only been here a week," said Harry.

"We could make a camp . . ."

"Done it," he countered.

"A tree-house!"

"Over on the far side, next to the footpath that goes up to the council houses," said Lara. "Last summer. Sorry." She smiled.

"Don't be so negative," wailed Emily. "We could spend all summer in this garden. We could camp here. Overnight as well . . ."

"Huh," said Jamie. "And you could try finding your way back in the middle of the night when Ellen decided she was frightened of the dark, or she wanted to go to the lavatory."

"I wouldn't," said Ellen, full of indignation. "You're the one who likes the light on at night. And you can talk; Mum said you were still wetting your bed when you were—"

Jamie's hand shot out and swept past her ear as she ducked. He would have tried again; but for the sound of Feather barking at the edge of the bushes.

The dog was scratching at the earth, its nose to the ground, bottom up, forelegs down, tail wagging.

"He's found something," said Jamie, getting up. "Leave," he commanded. "Leave it."

Feather continued to worry under the bush. Jamie grabbed him by the scruff of the neck and pulled him gently aside, peering in. "It's a hedgehog."

He crouched over a curled ball of spines. "Wow, they're sharp. Someone get a stick."

Harry brought a dead branch. Jamie used it to roll the curled hedgehog into the open.

"Be careful!" said Lara. "You'll hurt it with that."

"Course I won't." He rolled the hedgehog more or less into the centre of the clearing. He was still restraining Feather, who was whining and worrying to get near it.

"You won't like it," Ellen consoled him. "It's prickly and full of fleas."

"How do you know?" said Emily.

"I've got a book."

They took up their positions again, in a circle. This time the centrepiece was the hedgehog. Sounds nestled on Emily's lap.

"If we wait a bit it should unroll," said Jamie, trying to coax Feather to silence.

"I wonder what they eat?" said Emily. "Maybe we could keep it."

"Slugs," volunteered Ellen. "It's got a picture in my book."

"Urgh. I'm not collecting them."

"Be quiet, or it'll never unroll," Jamie ordered.

Emily ignored him. "I've been here a week and we've found a cat, a hedgehog—"

She stopped. A thought was forming. The hedgehog was beginning to unroll, but she didn't notice. The thought exploded into brilliance in her head.

She stood up, holding Sounds. "Hey, listen, I've got it."

"Oh, Emily! It's curled up again," shouted Jamie. "Be quiet!"

"No really, listen. I've got a great idea. Brilliant. And we can make some money, too."

"Tell us later."

"No, look . . ." She kneeled and grabbed Lara's arm. "Look, let's start a zoo. Our own zoo." The others watched as she bounced up and walked, ran nearly, from one to the other.

"We've got a rabbit, and a hedgehog, and Feather and Scab. We can make pens for them and sell things to feed them. I bet there's loads of kids who would come, specially the smaller ones."

"To get torn apart by Scab," chimed in Harry.

"We can get some wire and make him a big sort of cage," continued Emily, undaunted. "He won't be in it all the time. Only when we open.

"We'll write a notice: Danger, Wildcat. That'll make it more exciting. We can sell chocolate drops for the kids to feed him."

"It's a nice idea," murmured Lara, rising to her knees as her interest was aroused. "But four animals is hardly a zoo."

"We'll call it a wildlife park," said Emily. "We

can have trails with arrows. What about the tree-house – it's a jungle lookout. And I bet we could get more animals. I had a friend before we moved who wanted me to look after her mice while she was on holiday. I could get them and—"

"I've got two goldfish," said Harry. "If we could make a pond . . ."

Emily counted off on her fingers. "That's six altogether. And if we make some money maybe we can buy something proper, like in a real wildlife park. Oh, come on. It's a great idea. Look!"

The hedgehog had unrolled and was trundling across the clearing. Harry headed it off and it immediately curled into a ball. "We can sell other things. Like Emily said. Oats for the rabbit, fish-food for the goldfish," he said.

"Dog biscuits for Feather," added Lara.

Emily grinned. It hadn't taken long at all. They had begun by trying to argue her out of it; now they were arguing themselves into it. She grabbed the advantage.

"First thing is to make a pen for the hedgehog. We've got a crate some of our stuff came in. That should do it. I'll see if I can sneak it out without Dad seeing."

She was about to dash off when Jamie called, "Hold it!"

She turned back at the edge of the clearing, biting her lip. Why was he so . . . bullying! She feared he might wreck the whole enterprise and the words came out before she could stop them. "Is it because you don't like me personally, or do you enjoy being a

26

drag?" She tried to make it sound like a joke, but her voice carried an unmistakeable edge of sincerity.

Jamie flushed deeply, offended. "Listen you; all you've done since you got here is try to take over. We've been fine up to now. We don't need it. If you must know I was going to say we haven't got a name for the hedgehog yet; any ideas?"

It was Emily's turn to crimson. "I'm sorry. But you haven't exactly invented the perfect welcome, you know. You say practically nothing, and when you do speak it's, well . . . you talk more nicely to Feather! It's a great idea and you know it, so don't—"

Lara intervened. "Shut up, the pair of you. He's too cautious and you're too sensitive and if you don't call a truce soon you're in danger of wrecking a whole summer. It *is* a great idea. Even if it doesn't make a penny it'll give us something to do; and I quite fancy having my own menagerie." She looked at Emily, changing the subject rapidly. "You'll get used to him. And he's quite right; the hedgehog hasn't got a name. The zoo was your idea; you choose it."

Emily's irritation died like an itch scratched. She thought for a moment and a wide beam spread across her face. "Cuddles," she said, as she turned and ran for the path home.

Over the next few days they worked frantically. An uneasy truce settled between Emily and Jamie. He found a hammer and nails to build a pen for Cuddles. Two large roof slates formed a pitched roof for shelter and they stuffed it full of dry leaves. They read in Ellen's book that hedgehogs ate meat and they took turns to sneak out scraps of raw mince, and little bits of chops and joints from the parents' kitchens.

The rabbit hutch was moved into the clearing. Jamie forced open the ivy-clad shed and, hardly believing their luck, they found the remains of a roll of chicken wire which they used to make a run for Sounds.

The white mice, when they came, were easy. Their cage sat on a workbench in the shed, where Scab sat and watched them with an all-consuming hunger. At night they threw Scab out and secured the shed with a bent nail through the ancient hasp and staple catch.

Harry, Lara and Emily dug a pond for Harry's goldfish. They marked out a site as big as a bath, but a whole weary, sweaty day later their ambition had been whittled down to a hole the size of a kitchen sink. They lined it with polythene borrowed from Lara's mother (who never knew it had gone). The goldfish, with plants and water snails from their aquarium, were all transferred to the new home.

Feather was a problem. "I'm not having him tied up all day," said Jamie. "He'll just bark until we let him go. And a pen would need to be two metres high."

Emily came up with the answer. "Tie him on a long line and between times the kids can pay to take him for walks round the garden on the lead; he'll love it."

They all climbed up to last year's tree-house, testing its strength and tying on lengths of stout branch to make it safe. Below it in white emulsion on the smooth trunk a label read:

JUNGLE LOOKOUT

with an arrow pointing straight up.

Emily studied it thoughtfully before adding in smaller letters:

(at own risk)

They cleared pathways through the denser undergrowth where cardboard labels proclaimed: This way to the Rodents; This way to the Aquarium.

A chestnut tree had a card nailed to it stating its latin name: *Castenea sativa*.

Lara looked up the latin for hedgehog and wrote a notice: This way to the *erinaceus*.

They couldn't think how to contain Scab until Lara's father threw out an ancient dining table. They stood it in the clearing and nailed chicken wire around the legs, enclosing the space beneath. Emily coaxed Scab on to the grass while the others placed the table over him. He growled suspiciously, despite offerings of milk and cat food.

Ellen pushed a sympathetic finger through the mesh and he lashed irritably at it. She was quick enough to retract her hand undamaged.

"He's never going to stand strangers," groaned Emily, shaking her head. They placed a boundary rope round the table a metre from it and hung a notice proclaiming:

Wildcat.
Dangerous Animal.
Do not cross barrier.

They walked round together, examining their work, making minor adjustments. Little bags of nuts and raisins, borrowed from larders, were ready for feeding mice. Feather's dog biscuits were offered for sale.

"They can throw them up for him. Really high. He's great at catching them," said Jamie proudly.

But with the opening imminent it was Emily who began to have doubts. "Maybe you were right," she said, staring down at the faint orange blur of the two goldfish in their pond. Maybe we don't have enough.

Lara gave her a nudge. "What! It's great." She counted off on her fingers. "We've got two mice and a wild cat; a rabbit and a dog which they can actually handle in the pets corner, two goldfish, and an *erinaceus*. We reckon it's brilliant, don't we?" She nodded to the others, rallying their support. Only Jamie remained non-committal.

"All the same," said Emily, sucking thoughtfully at her lower lip, "A little bit more wouldn't hurt.

"If only we could find something else; just one. Something really wild . . ."

30

Three

The following day they planned to tour the neighbourhood telling children the zoo opening was imminent. Emily was excused, partly because she didn't know many other children, and because she made the mistake of popping back to the house for more paint to write signs.

"That's lucky," said her mother. "Once you get in that garden I never seem to see you. I'd like you to pop down to the shops and get some washing powder."

"Oh, Mum!"

"Oh nothing. Do it, please."

"But I'm busy . . ."

"Me too; that's why you're going. Here's the money. Don't forget to wait for the change."

Emily sulked all the way. Returning home she spent her annoyance on the carrier bag, swinging it out in front of her and kicking the packet inside as it swung down again.

As she rounded a corner she heard noises: a babble of excited voices all trying to be heard.

"It was here . . ."

"I saw it over here . . ."

"It came down a bit further—"

"Don't push."

Along the suburban street hedges topped low garden walls. Bunched in one section, shoving and searching through the foliage, was a crowd of children of all ages.

As Emily approached, a young girl separated from the others and ran past her, turning in through an open gate.

Emily stopped her. "What's going on?"

"Someone's shot a bird; with an air rifle. It flew down into the hedge but we can't find it. I'm going to look on the inside." She dashed off, calling after her, "It's still alive, we think."

Emily watched another figure break free. "What a shot, eh?" The face looked around for agreement. Emily felt her stomach churn as she recognized Mark, the boy who had been with Sean.

Then a bigger figure straightened up out of the crowd. Sean. He was still holding the air rifle, using the length of it to shove the younger children aside.

"If you lot would just keep out of my way, I could find it," he roared. "And don't forget – it's mine. I shot it; I want it."

Emily turned away. Disgust showed clearly on her face, but she was fearful in case Sean recognized her while she was alone and vulnerable. He was too busy to notice. He shoved another child aside and began poking furiously into the hedge with the butt of the rifle, intent on his prey.

Emily kept walking, her knuckles white where she gripped the bag, her pulse beating so hard she could feel it in her ears. She was obliged to step off the kerb to walk round the crowd. She stepped up again and continued on her way.

When she had gone some twenty metres she heard a brief scrabbling beside her in the hedge. She hesitated and looked, and the noise stopped. She began again, and the sound returned briefly: a noise like mice in dry leaves. She slowed and stopped, peering cautiously behind her. The crowd still squealed, pressing forward over one another into the hedge. Emily peered closer into the foliage.

At first she saw nothing. The shadows behind the leaves were unyielding and shapeless; but as she stared her eyes grew familiar with the shade, until she could pick out the dry twig stems that made up the hedge's interior. Among them she saw a bright, dark eye that shone back at her like a black bead. It moved to watch her better, and she made out a shape: a heavy beak, and a large black body shining like polish in the shadows. It was a crow.

She stole a quick glance backwards. One or two of the crowd had broken away and were peering into the hedges nearer her.

She chewed nervously at her lip. "They're going to find you," she whispered.

She joggled the bag noisily in its direction. "Go on. Shoo! Run; fly!" Then she added sadly, "I bet you can't, can you?"

More children had broken away from the main group. Emily took a deep breath, and put down the carrier bag. She placed it carefully so she could pick it up again with one hand.

33

She reached stealthily into the hedge until she felt her fingers touch the hard, smooth gloss of the feathers. The bird tried to move away, but before it could do so her hands closed round it. Carefully she pulled it through the foliage, taking care not to snag the feathers on the twigs as it appeared tail first, its wings snugly secure in her hands.

She was shielding her actions from the children with her back. She took another glance at them. One, the nearest, was only a few metres away. He was a small boy not much older than Ellen, and he was watching her curiously.

She turned away, adjusting her grip so she could hold the crow comfortably in one arm and reach for the bag. The boy was walking towards her. She scooped up the bag and walked smartly away. The boy quickened his pace, too, uncertain.

"What's that?" he called tentatively.

Emily heard a voice calling in her thoughts, "Slow down, slow down . . . don't panic." But her feet wouldn't listen to it. Her steps grew more rapid.

"Hey!" he called. "Have you got it?"

She stumbled into a run, and then he knew.

"It's here!" he yelled to the others. "It's here. Quick. She's taking it!"

Emily was already thirty metres away. The boy yelled again. One or two heads straightened out of the bushes and looked in his direction. Emily was nearing the corner at the far end of the street. The younger children were tugging at Sean's sleeve.

Eventually their message got through. He looked up and followed their gaze.

Emily looked back. As she turned Sean glimpsed the gloss of black feathers tucked under her arm. With a roar of rage he raced through the crowd, just as she turned the far end of the street, fifty metres away. She was already breathless, clenching her teeth with effort, when she heard the roar and whoop of the pack as they raced in pursuit.

Maybe she could outrun most of the others, she wasn't sure; but she knew Sean was faster. He would catch her in a straight race for home – but she had a head start.

She was one street away. The length of it stretched ahead and she ran clumsily, bird in one hand, bag in the other. Her breath began to wheeze in her lungs. Just one more corner, and the run to the far end of her own street, and she would be safe. Maybe the others would be there and would run to her aid.

The crowd cleared the corner behind her. She looked back and felt her heart slam in panic against her chest. Sean was already well ahead. He was halfway between them and her, the air rifle gripped in one hand, his jaw set and his face red with effort. The rapid, rhythmic pounding of his feet marked his speed.

Emily gasped for air, breath crackling in her throat as she forced her stumbling legs forward. She fled onwards, not daring to look back, when she heard Sean swear and the gasp of a woman's voice.

A pram had appeared from a gateway and Sean swerved out of its path, catching it with his arm as he passed. The pram lurched violently. Emily heard a baby cry, and the woman yell in indignation. Emily looked back to see Sean recover. The gap between them had widened a little. Further back, beyond the pram, the rest of the crowd was strung out as the slower ones fell behind.

She swept round the last corner, her hair flicking at the hedge as she passed blindly into her own street. She was heedless of anything that might lie in her path. Her speed carried her off the pavement, plunging into the road as she rounded the bend.

She could see her gate – middle one of the three – and the first-floor windows of the three tall, Victorian houses and she sobbed inwardly. They seemed so small, so distant; and there was no sign of Jamie or the others – not even Ellen – to whom she could shout for help.

Sean's footfalls thudded in her ears as he hurtled round the corner behind her.

Her flagging muscles and tortured breath took their toll. The rhythm went out of her strides and she faltered, nearly fell, recovered and ran on. Sean was gaining quickly now. She could hear the laboured rasp of his breath. Still the gate seemed a long way off. Her breath rattled in her throat, and a dry rasp began to bite into her chest as it pumped and fought for more speed.

"If I can get through," she thought. "If I can reach the front door . . . he wouldn't dare do anything, not with Mum there."

The crow and the bag were deadweights. As exhaustion overtook her the swinging bag banged her legs, almost throwing her down. She couldn't call out now, no matter who had been near; her mouth was gummed with a sticky mucous that stopped her even from swallowing. She was nearly level with the first gate – Jamie's – set in its high, unruly hedge. She snatched a glance backwards, and nearly fell with shock. Sean was so close his arm was stretched out to grab her.

She found an extra spurt from a dark, terrified corner inside her. Sean, too, was tiring. The gap widened briefly before Sean also recovered. There were only a few metres to the gate, a few strides; ten, less than ten, when the sickening realization came to Emily that it was hopeless.

The gate was latched. Her parents, who would leave a door half-painted for twelve months, had mended the gate latch the day after they moved in. "Start as we mean to go on," her father had said as he clicked the gate shut.

Now she slammed into it with a rattling crash. She held the crow high to protect it from the impact, and in the same instant she span round to face Sean, her teeth gritted with effort and defiance. The carrier bag swung round with her as she turned. Sean thundered across the last two metres and the weight of the washing powder in its carton caught him a smacking blow in the ribs.

The surprise made him swerve into the thick hedge. He stopped with his shoulders pumping; his head sagged as he desperately gulped air into his lungs. Emily was in the same state; her knees nearly buckling and a searing, dry pain across her chest as her lungs and heart pumped relentlessly.

She saw a thin chance. Exhausted and trembling as she was, she reached for the latch. Sean beat her to it. He reached over and covered it, careful to remain out of sight from anyone who might watch from the windows.

"Stupid . . ." he gasped, competing for the words against the urgent need of his straining lungs. "Give it . . . here . . ."

Emily shook her head, unable to find breath for words. Her mouth was filled with the dry acid taste of bile. All she could do was support herself against the gate, while she held the crow protected on the side furthest from Sean.

He shoved her. "Give . . . 'smine . . ." He held out his hand. Again she shook her head, her legs quivering in a desperate effort to hold her up. She looked round for help. There was no-one about; not James, nor Lara, nor her mother. The rest of the strung-out crowd was arriving, gasping for breath.

Sean gestured towards them. "They saw," he gasped, gulping in air as his breath slowly returned to him. "Great shot. Wasn't it?" He grinned into the crowd, nodding, seeking their approval.

"Yeah!" shouted Mark. Emily saw Chrissie beside him, echoing his approval.

Emily's breath was a crackling wheeze in her throat as she looked up at the rest of them. "He'll only . . . kill it. Why d'you think he . . . shot it." Her lip curled in disgust. She added sarcastically, "So's he can give it a good home?"

The crowd was silent, looking to Sean for an answer. He turned towards them. "None of her business. I shot it, didn't I? 'Smine." He clenched his fist, still hunched round the stock of the air rifle, and held it under Emily's nose. "Listen; just give it here, or you'll get this."

Emily backed into the closed gate. As she did so she heard a familiar sound. Scab jumped, mewing, from the far side of the gate on to its top rail. He rubbed himself sinuously against Emily's shoulder. Her voice cracked with relief that was close to tears. "Oh Scab, Scab. Oh thank you," she cried. The cat climbed forward on to Emily's shoulder and stood kneading with its claws. He surveyed first the crow and then Sean through angry green slits.

Sean backed away. The movement was indiscernible to the rest of the crowd but it wasn't lost on Emily. He raised his fist again, with the gun in it. Scab showed his teeth and spat angrily.

Emily had no idea how much damage an air rifle could do, but she remembered Sean's threat. She turned slightly, trying to shield both the crow and Scab from the weapon. Sean saw the movement and brought the gun round to bear on her. "I've already warned you about that cat," he snarled. "Now why don't you just hand over the bird, or—"

Another figure appeared in the gateway and Sean stopped in surprise. It was Lara; Harry came into view behind her. Lara was younger than Sean by two years, but if she was frightened by him she didn't show it.

She smiled at Emily and turned to address Sean. "Or what, Sean Beddock? You'll kill Scab? If you could've done that you would have already."

She turned to Emily. "He knows he shouldn't have a gun in the street. It's against the law."

She eyed Sean seriously. "It's probably not even loaded." She saw in his face she had guessed right and a slow smile spread across her face.

Sean snarled. "She hit me. No-one does that." He gave Emily a shove that nearly overbalanced her into the hedge. Stumbling, she retained her hold on the struggling crow. Scab screamed and struck out at Sean. Lara whispered to Harry who nodded and ran away out of sight. She opened the gate and ducked past Sean to Emily's side. "Leave her alone. She hasn't done anything."

"She hit me with that!" stormed Sean, pointing at the bag. "And she's got my bird. I shot it. It's mine!"

The thin whine of Chrissie's voice sounded from the edge of the crowd. "Give it back to Sean; he won't kill it. He didn't mean to hurt it."

Sean was nodding his agreement and there were a few murmurs of approval.

With Lara beside her Emily's courage returned and her legs and voice came back under control. She had an idea. "Look, he's already shot it, so he must've been trying to. Maybe it's dying already." She held it up for them to see. The crow's head sank back into its neck as it was exposed to view. "And what does he want it for? Keep it in a cage, I bet. I'll take care of it, and while it's recovering you can all come and see it."

There was silence. "We're starting a zoo round the back. Like a wildlife park. You know, with animals and birds and things."

She watched their eyes. They were taking the bait; she could read the interest in their faces.

Just to be sure she added, "Like Longleat."

From the corner of her eye she saw Lara's head swivel towards her and her mouth open, eyes popping.

Longleat was a stately home in the English country-side; the grand residence of Lord Bath. Everyone knew about it. Her parents had promised to take her there, though they still had not done so. The vast grounds of the estate had been turned into a wildlife park; a real wildlife park with lions, giraffes, monkeys . . .

"What?" called a voice. "With lions and things, like Longleat?"

Emily took a deep breath. No stopping now. "Yes," she said, ignoring Lara's shocked look.

"It's opening tomorrow." She indicated the crow, still under one arm. "As soon as it's fit enough – if he hasn't killed it, that is," she nodded dismissively towards Sean who glowered angrily. "As soon as it's fit you can all come and visit us before we let it go."

She surveyed the eager eyes around her and added, "Hey, it hasn't got a name. What shall we call it?"

Beside her Lara smiled as she watched Emily drawing them in with her enthusiasm. They had forgotten now that ownership was in question. The only question was the name.

Jamie appeared in the gateway, fetched by Harry. Feather was grinning at his heels. Sean scowled and Jamie blushed, but they both stood and listened while the names came:

"Blackie."

"Beak."

"Dracula."

"Yes, Dracula. That's it!"

The vote went for Dracula.

"Dracula it is," called Emily. "Keep your fingers crossed that he gets well."

Sean opened his mouth to speak, and made a gesture at Emily. Scab growled and spat from her arms, ears laid back. Jamie moved quickly through the gates with Feather. Sean stopped and looked around. The mob that had followed him was silent, watching critically. His confidence was gone now he no longer felt the strength of the crowd behind him. With a growl of anger he strode away, elbowing a small child out of his patch, barging through the rest, and stamping away up the street. Mark and Chrissie detached themselves sheepishly from the others and followed quickly after him.

They were soon forgotten as the remainder turned back to Emily. She was busy prising Scab away from Dracula. With Sean gone the cat was showing an unhealthy interest in the crow.

"So what sort of animals will there be?"

"Oh, lots," said Emily casually, changing the subject. "And you can feed them. And there's other things, too. We've got jungle walks, and a treehouse . . ."

Lara was whispering to Jamie. Emily could see from his dropping jaw that she was telling him the Longleat story. She turned her attention back to the crowd of children, indicating the crow.

"Anyway, we'd better get this poor thing somewhere we can have a look at it. See you tomorrow. Don't forget some money to get in and to buy some food for the animals."

She bounced in through the gate and lowered Scab to the floor where he sat looking up, fixing Dracula with a cold stare.

Without waiting for the others she ran off around the side of the houses to the back garden with Scab in pursuit. She struggled through the undergrowth, carefully shielding the crow from brambles and

43

branches, until she reached the shed. Inside she dropped the carrier bag and the washing powder to the floor and shoved the door, squeaking and scraping it shut before Scab could squeeze through. She put the crow down on the work top. In one corner the mice scuttled across their cage into the nesting box. She could see a nose quivering at the entrance.

The crow shook its ruffled feathers. "Kaark," it called tentatively. Emily watched. It hopped along the bench until it reached the end and launched itself off the edge. One wing drooped and the bird fluttered to the floor. It hopped clumsily into a corner where Emily scooped it up and placed it back on the work surface. Carefully she lifted the wing. There was no sign of damage, and the bird did not complain. Instead it turned its dark, gleaming eye on Emily's hand and stabbed with its broad beak.

"Ouch!" she yelled. "Thanks a bunch. I think I'll give you back, you great—"

The door burst open and the others shot in. First, Lara, then Harry, Jamie and Ellen. The bird reacted with a single wild, "Kraark!" before flapping high into the pitch of the roof.

Harry eyed the crow. "Doesn't seem to be much wrong with that."

Emily agreed, nursing her pecked hand. "If it had been hit you'd think there would be blood or something."

"They've got incredibly hard feathers," volunteered Lara. "Maybe the shock just winded it."

"Well, we'd better keep him a couple of days,

just to be sure," said Emily. She counted off on her fingers. "So, that's Feather, Scab, the hedgehog, Sounds, two goldfish, two mice and now . . . Dracula. That's nine. I reckon we're ready. Don't you?"

She looked up, unable to avoid Jamie's eyes. They blazed down at her. "Don't give us that. Just what were you doing with all that Longleat stuff?"

She looked to the others. They weren't smiling. "Lions?" said Lara. "Giraffes? Monkeys?"

"Oh, they won't expect to see them. I was just explaining about wildlife parks." Emily tried to change the subject. "So where can we put Dracula?"

"Emily," gasped Lara, indignantly. "You told them we had lions and things. What are they going to say tomorrow; when they see we don't? Why do you have to go over the top? You can't blame Jamie if—"

"I'm sorry," Emily cut in sheepishly. "But we had to get them on our side. You could see that, couldn't you? And that stupid boy . . . we couldn't let him take Dracula. We couldn't . . ." She looked round for support.

Harry shook his head. "You're a liability," he said; but there was a strong note of admiration in his voice.

"I hit him," said Emily. "With Mum's washing powder."

Jamie shook his head. "You *are* a liability."

"He was awful. And . . . well, I just got carried away. Sorry."

45

She looked crestfallen for a moment, before bouncing up and down excitedly on the spot. "And we have got a zoo now: fish, birds, rodents, mammals . . . who needs giraffes? You'll see, it won't matter."

Four

Dracula didn't seem hurt, and if he wasn't hurt it wasn't fair to keep him shut in the shed. They borrowed on their next week's pocket money and pooled the cash to buy nylon garden netting. Using a stepladder they hung the netting in the trees, making a large, enclosed aviary.

"If no-one comes we're going to be seriously broke," grumbled Jamie as he folded the stepladder and carted it back to the house. Emily and the others stood watching the crow in his new home.

"They'll come," replied Emily absently.

When Jamie returned they surveyed their handiwork. Painted boards drying in the sun proclaimed feeding times, and guided walks, and a wildcat (*dangerous; do not feed*). Cuddles waddled out of his nest of leaves and snuffled over to a dish of minced meat. He had grown familiar with the children's noise and rarely curled into a ball in their presence. The goldfish basked in the sunlight while Scab watched hungrily through half-closed eyes, feigning sleep, and Dracula splashed noisily in an old-fashioned china sink that Harry had dragged from the far side of the three gardens to provide water in the aviary.

"Okay," said Emily. "When do we start?"

"Tomorrow, tomorrow, tomorrow," chanted Ellen, dancing round the others.

Lara shook her head doubtfully, kicking at a grassblade. "Are we ready, though?"

Emily swept an arm round the clearing, indicating the pets and the signs. "What else can we do? We can't be any readier than this."

She held out her flat hand to Ellen, palm side up, and her infectious grin spread over her face. "I'm with Ellen. Tomorrow."

Ellen slapped the offered hand and yelled, "Yippee!"

Lara stepped forward and slapped it, too, returning Emily's grin. Harry followed. Jamie looked at the offered hand and pretended he hadn't seen it. He hastily put his hands in his pockets and walked away, his face red. Emily flushed, shaking her head with a sigh. She didn't understand; she liked people to like her; she was more hurt than offended. She set her jaw. "I'm not giving up," she thought. "Not yet, anyway."

Next day they were out early feeding the animals, and placing signs. Scab was enticed under the table-cage with a tin of catfood. Only after he had wolfed it down did he realize he'd been tricked. He sat in the middle of the floor with his back to everyone, scowling and flicking the kink in the end of his tail. Feather, tongue lolling and tail wagging expectantly, was tied to a long leash. A sign above him proclaimed: *Dog Walks. Five Pence.*

Ellen was delighted to be placed in charge of collecting entrance money at the side gate. When they erected the signs there were already four children waiting. She bossed them unmercifully, though they were twice her age. "You have to make a straight line. Go on. One at a time. Why haven't you got the right money? Shall I let him in Emily, if he hasn't got the right money?"

Emily, Lara and Harry spluttered behind their hands as the visitors meekly presented their coins to Ellen, who had to stand on tip-toe to see into her cashbox: a converted biscuit tin on top of a black-painted upturned crate.

Jamie groaned, "No-one's going to come if she goes on like that."

"Doesn't seem to be bothering this lot," said Emily, laughing. "Come on. We're on duty."

As they ran back to the clearing other children were already joining the queue. Lara was to police the goldfish, the mice in the garden shed, and Cuddles; while Emily cared for Sounds – who was offered for five pence a hold – and for the unwitting children who were inclined to ignore the warnings and approach too close to Scab's enclosure.

Jamie refused to let anyone else be responsible for Feather. Throughout the day he fussed over younger children who were eager to take the dog for a walk round the specially arrowed path through the garden's wilderness. "Are you sure you can hold him. He's strong. Don't worry if he jumps up at you. He just wants to play. Put the lead through

49

your hand like this. Don't tug at him. *He* knows what he's doing."

While Feather was being walked Jamie supervised children who scrambled precariously over the tree-house, warning them, "Use two hands. No, not that way. Be careful behind you. There! I told you he'd get kicked in the face. Are you all right? No, it's not bleeding."

Harry took charge of Dracula. He alternated between herding small groups into the aviary and supervising guided walks round the garden's overgrown paths. In the aviary the crow eyed them suspiciously while Harry told stories, heavily embellished, of its rescue from death.

On the walks he showed them the carcase of a dead, dried frog, and how to make itching powder from rosehips when the roses died at the end of the summer. To their fascination (and Harry's) they found a dead starling infested with black ants, marching continuously in and out of the body. The children huddled around it while Harry, because he was in charge, assumed the right to turn it over with a stick.

All day the children came. No-one realized lunch-time had passed until Ellen appeared, furious, clutch-ing her biscuit tin and followed by a line of bewildered children.

She stamped her feet. "I'm hungry and thirsty and I'm not playing unless I can have something to eat."

They persuaded her to return to the gate while they fetched a snack.

The bags of animal food diminished: dog biscuits and dried nuts and bits of cheese and stale bread for the mice, dandelion leaves for Sounds.

One boy found a slug and was awarded the privilege of feeding it free to Cuddles, who made short work of it to the fascination and horror of everyone.

Much later Ellen returned, again clutching her tin. "We haven't had anyone for ages and I've counted the money loads of times. I want to do something else."

"You can't count," said Jamie, ignoring the face she pulled. "But it is getting late. Maybe we'd better stop and see how we've done."

Once the last lingering child had been coaxed out of the garden they sat in the fading light and counted the money.

"Three pounds, twenty pence," proclaimed Lara, after she had checked it.

"That's what I made it," said Ellen, but no-one was listening.

Jamie whistled. "That's more than all our pocket money put together, all in one day."

"We've got to take out what we spent on food for the animals," Lara reminded him, "but even then it's more than I thought."

"And me." Emily picked up a pile of coins and let them run through her fingers, dreamily. "Really good," she crooned.

"And we can do it again tomorrow, and the next day, and the next day," called Harry from the aviary, where Dracula sat on a branch accepting

51

bits of Cuddles' left-over mince from the boy's fingers.

"I wonder if we'll get as many?" said Jamie to himself.

Days passed and every evening they asked themselves the same question; every morning the queues had already begun when they opened the gate. They added a rope swing to the treehouse; a girl who was going abroad for the remainder of the summer holiday asked them to look after her guinea pig. Gratefully they agreed, and placed the hutch beside Sounds'.

The contents of the biscuit tin multiplied. Lara organized an exercise book of accounts showing how much they were spending on food and bedding, and how much money they were making.

Harry conducted the guided walk so many times he was saying it in his sleep. The dead starling decayed into the earth and he searched out another delight: a rat's skeleton held together by dried, board-hard skin. He discovered it on the topmost dusty shelf in the garden shed.

He was at the door of the shed, proudly showing it to an open-mouthed group as the finale to the third guided walk that morning, when he heard voices raised and Ellen's inimitable shriek of indignance. It was followed by a raucous laugh.

He pushed through the group and ran to the clearing. Jamie was on the far side. Beside him, weeping uncontrollably into his hip, was Ellen. Jamie had one arm round her and his face was flushed with anger. In front of him, his back to

Harry, was another bigger boy. It didn't matter that Harry couldn't see his face. He knew the voice.

"How do I know if I wanna pay until I've seen it?" the voice mocked.

It was Sean. To one side were his two followers, Mark and Chrissie, wearing their inane sneers as usual. Emily and Lara were standing to one side, stony-faced and silent.

"That's no reason to go shoving my sister around," said Jamie, the words coming out pinched and full of fury.

Sean swung round. His eyes took in Feather, who was growling softly, secured at the end of his tether, and the inscrutable Scab, who sat penned under the table. There was a smirk on the boy's face. "What're you goin' to do about it?" he challenged.

A few children had gathered cautiously at the edges of the clearing, and were listening to the confrontation.

"So let's see what you've got in this . . . zoo!" Sean spat the words out scornfully as he swaggered round the clearing. "Let's see just what's worth payin' for – or is it just a rip-off, eh?"

He stopped in front of Harry. The smaller boy's knees trembled. He didn't dare challenge Sean's menacing eyes; but he stood his ground, head down, hands clenched at his sides, still holding the mummified rat carcase.

Sean roared with laughter, and with a swift movement snatched the rat away from Harry. He held it up for everyone to see. "This one's not even alive!" he chortled. "You have to pay to see dead animals, do you?"

Sean walked over to Scab's pen. The cat viewed him through slit eyes, drew back its lips in a snarl, but Sean knew he was safe.

"Well, a little pussy cat. Puss, puss, puss." He read out loud the words on the board that stood beside the wire: "Wild Cat. Dangerous Animal. Do not cross barrier." He scoffed. "That's not a wild cat. That's an old stray tom that comes and does its wassnames in my mum's garden."

Scab snarled noiselessly at him. Sean moved on to the two hutches, side by side. "And what have we here? More dead animals?" The guinea pig was out of sight, but Sounds hopped back from the wire as Sean spoke. "Oh no; this one's still alive." He stood upright and the false grin changed to a menace. "Still, we can always do something about that, can't we?"

Emily moved forward, restrained by Lara. "You leave him alone," she glared, her voice trembling. Sean's eyes lit up and she knew she had given away too much.

"So this one's yours eh? Well, well." He moved back round the circle one more time, stopping as he did so in front of all the animals, but taking care to keep beyond the reach of Feather's tether. "So this is it: a mangy dog . . . a scabby tom." He moved round to Cuddle's pen and kicked a board flat. Luckily the hedgehog had retired to its nest and was not in sight. "A hedgehog you can't see . . ." He toed the slates apart and they fell aside. Cuddles, exposed suddenly to view, immediately curled into a ball.

"That's better," roared Sean with delight.

He moved on the pond. "A goldfish . . ." The second fish swam into view. "Ah, I do apologize," he said theatrically. "*Two* goldfish. Excuse me." He tossed in the rat carcase. "Suppertime, fishes!" he called, cackling at his own joke.

No-one moved as he continued round the clearing. "What's in here?" He tore the netting apart and leapt back suddenly as the startled Dracula flapped wildly on his branch and cried, "Kraark, kaark, kaark!"

"My crow," he growled.

He returned to the hutches. "A guinea pig . . . a dozy rabbit . . ."

He strolled round to where Emily stood with Lara still holding on to her arm. He rocked slightly on his heels, his arms loose by his side, his eyes penetrating Emily, who stared silently back, her eyes full of hatred.

". . . and you!" he ended. His arm shot out and his fingers locked into Emily's hair. The two girls shrieked in alarm and Lara beat at Sean's arm. His other hand cuffed her heavily round the ear, sending her sprawling. He turned back to Emily, pulling her down until she lost her footing. Her hands fumbled blindly for his wrists as she fell. "I'll teach you to cross me!" he spat, his lip curled back.

"I won't cry," thought Emily. "I mustn't cry." She was grateful that her head was down so no-one could see how close she was to tears. She bit at her bottom lip and fought to hold his wrist closer to her head, to ease the pain from the tension on her hair. Suddenly he let go.

She heard a muffled gasp, "Uh!" as the wind was driven from his body, and when she looked up he was sprawled on the grass with Jamie standing over him.

Feather barked and pulled at his tether, but he was securely tied. Sean was up in an instant. As Jamie reached down to help Emily to her feet, Sean's fist swung up in a savage arc. Lara and Ellen screamed, Feather went wild with impotent fury on his leash.

No-one saw Harry as he sidled towards the enraged dog. Their eyes were on Jamie. He had seen Sean's arm swing and dodged – too late. The first struck the edge of Jamie's nose and scorched across his cheek, leaving a livid mark. He clutched his face as blood bubbled from a nostril.

Ellen screamed again and rushed across the clearing. She flung herself round Jamie's legs, weeping freely but undeterred as Sean raised his fist again.

Harry had reached Feather. With his hands on the dog's collar, he yelled, "No! I'll let him go. Get out; or I will."

Sean halted abruptly in mid-swing.

The dog was straining against Harry's hold, baring its teeth and snarling a heavy, deadly growl that ran on until he snatched a breath, and then began again.

Sean lowered his fist and backed away. "What's

56

the odds," he said. "Don't know what we're doing in this crummy place anyway."

He swung round to his two cronies, whose faces were now pale and nervous. "Let's get out of here." They followed him out of the clearing.

As he went he kicked out at the rabbit hutch. One of its legs buckled and the whole hutch toppled forward on to its front with a sickening crunch. The rabbit squealed with terror, hidden within.

"Sounds!" screamed Emily. "Sounds!" Tears burst through her self control and flowed down her buckled face as she tore at the heavy cage to turn it over.

Lara ran to help. The rabbit had stopped squealing; there was no sound from the hutch. Gradually they hauled it upright. Emily tore at the catch and flung open the door, sobbing uncontrollably. "Oh Sounds, I'm sorry. I'm sorry." She lifted the struggling rabbit out, quieting it with her arms as it trembled violently.

Her tears ran down the rabbit's fur, streaking it into matted points. Lara put her arm round the sobbing girl. "It's all right. Sean's gone now. Sounds will be okay. Look, give him some dandelion." She reached a stray leaf out of the hutch and presented it to Sounds, but the rabbit ignored it.

Emily continued to sob, pressing her face into its fur. "He'll . . . he'll be all right." she wept. "Look after Jamie."

Harry had let Feather go and the bewildered dog clawed at Jamie, who stood with his head held back, nursing his nose with a bloody hand, fending off Feather with the other. Lara dragged a handkerchief out of her jeans.

"Here," she said, "Use this. Get down Feather."

Jamie took the handkerchief and applied it to his bleeding nose. "Leab hib alone," he mumbled. "Leab me alone. Just shut up."

"Yes, leave him alone," sniffed Ellen, still clinging hard to Jamie's legs, her cheeks stained with tears.

"For Gob's sake Ellen, you'll hab me ober," mumbled Jamie through the handkerchief.

They all watched in silent sympathy as he dabbed at his nose and gingerly nursed his grazed cheek.

The children who had been watching at the edges of the clearing had melted away. Jamie gently unhooked Ellen from his legs and lowered himself to the ground. Feather leaped forward, whimpering and licking.

"Yuk," shrieked Ellen, "He's licking the blood! Urgh!"

Lara held Feather by the collar and made him sit. Harry rescued his rat skeleton from the fish pond and Emily, who had wiped her face dry of tears, shuffled over on her knees with Sounds, and sat sniffing as she watched Jamie.

"Thank you for what you did," she said. "I'm sorry you got bashed."

Jamie shrugged. The blood had stopped flowing, and he was dabbing at the last of it with the handkerchief, folding it to expose the few remaining clean places.

"So am I. Never mind. Maybe now he's got his revenge he'll leave us alone."

Lara snorted. "Don't count on it."

Jamie gave Harry a friendly shove with his foot.

"Thank you," he said. "If you hadn't got to Feather it might have been worse."

Harry flushed. "I'm sorry I didn't have a go at him myself." He kicked at the ground with his heel and looked up. "He's . . . he's a bit big for me."

Jamie managed a grin. "He's a bit big for all of us."

"Especially his mouth," muttered Emily, and they all laughed.

"Look," said Lara, "We've got to mend Sounds' hutch, and we're all feeling a bit wobbly. The visitors have taken fright; let's close now and have the rest of the day to ourselves. We've earned it."

Five

By eleven o'clock next morning not one person had paid their entrance money into Ellen's biscuit tin. She stamped crossly back from the gate to find the others sitting despondently in a circle in the clearing.

"Why hasn't anyone come?" she moaned. "I'm bored."

"So are we," said Emily. She eased herself from the ground and crossed over to the enclosure where Scab was sitting carefully preening one extended hind leg. She lifted the wire and left it open, but the cat took no notice.

Jamie unclipped Feather's lead from his collar. The graze on Jamie's cheek was still sore, but his nose had recovered. They agreed it was sensible not to have Feather permanently tied; instead Jamie had the lead in his hand in readiness for visitors.

"Maybe they're just frightened Sean might come back," offered Harry. "I would be if I was them."

"Huh!" sniffed Lara. "He's probably threatened to bash them all if they do."

A miserable silence hung over them. Emily sat down again with a sigh and lay on her stomach, her chin cupped in her hands. "I don't know; maybe he was right," she said gloomily. "Maybe it's not much of a zoo."

"How can you say that!" Harry looked up indignantly. "It's a great zoo. No-one else has complained. Some have even been back more than once."

"Yes, but it's a bit . . . well, tame. Isn't it? I mean, the most unusual thing we've got is a crow, and your dead rat."

"If only we had a real wild animal," added Lara. "Like a monkey or something."

Ellen held out the biscuit tin. "Let's buy one. We've got loads of money now."

"Don't be daft," said her brother. "You can't just go and buy animals like that. You have to have licenses and stuff."

"Do not!" yelled Ellen. "Lots of people have got them."

"Who?" challenged Jamie.

"Not telling you."

"See. You're a liar."

"Not."

Lara interrupted. "Oh, pack it in. Neither of you has a clue what you're talking about."

Jamie turned on his heel and strode out of the clearing. Lara sat upright, baffled. "Well, where's he gone?"

"Sulking," said Ellen. Mum says—"

"Shut up," said Lara.

Emily joined in. "He's all right. We'd have been in trouble yesterday without him."

Jamie appeared again through the bushes, carrying

a newspaper. He turned a few pages, and tossed it down in front of Lara, saying, "It was in the box in the shed; the one we keep with stuff for cleaning out the cages. I got reading it when I was doing the mice."

Lara picked it up. Jamie went on, "Just read that bit on the front to my dozy sister, will you?"

Lara scanned the page. She read:

PANTHER MAN APPEAL REJECTED

A 15-year old black panther must be destroyed unless a zoo can be found to house it, a judge ruled this week.

An appeal for a licence to keep the animal, reputed to be one of the most dangerous members of the cat family, was turned down at a special court hearing on Wednesday, despite the owner's claim it was "friendlier than a kitten".

Mr Bernard Mansard, of Knightswood Manor, said: "My children and my grandchildren love her. They have always been safe with her and we keep her secure behind high fences.

"In fifteen years I never knew I needed a licence. It's bad enough losing her to a zoo. If she has to be put down we'll be heartbroken.

"She has never escaped; I doubt if she would even want to. I don't see what the problem is."

Rejecting the appeal, Mr Justice Sloane said: "The public has a right to know it is safe from the threat of dangerous animals in urban areas.

"I regret that if a zoo cannot be found to take this

*creature within two weeks I will have no alternative
but to authorize its immediate destruction."*

Lara handed the paper back to Jamie who tapped
Ellen on the head with it twice, chanting as he did
so: "So . . . there."

Ellen poked her tongue out and turned away.

"Poor man," said Emily. "Fifteen years! It must
be just like a pet. Where's Knightswood Manor?"

Jamie tossed her the paper. "Oh, miles away. I
think. It's a big country mansion sort of place."

"Hey, listen to this." Emily's gaze had fallen on
another item. She read:

URBAN WILDLIFE UNDER THREAT

*A vixen killed by a car on Boundary road, near
the new Stanworth airport, was a mother who had
left her cubs to search for food, RSPCA inspector
Frank Hampson said yesterday.*

*"From her condition it was clear there was
at least one cub, probably more, that will die
of starvation in a den somewhere on the airport
perimeter," he said.*

*"So far we've searched the north, south and
east boundaries for them, but it's like looking for
a needle in a haystack."*

*He said the growth of urban wildlife, such as
foxes and badgers, was one of the great benefits of
inaccessible open spaces created by modern airport
development. But when creatures wandered away
from that environment in search of food they were*

63

in grave danger from fast-moving traffic.

Emily looked up. "That's only about five miles away. They're right under our noses!"

"Poor things," said Lara. "What a way to go; starving to death. And no mother."

"Pity we can't rescue them." said Harry.

Lara and Emily looked at him, and at each other. Each saw the same thought mirrored in the eyes of the other; and as that knowledge came to them a slow grin spread over their faces.

"We can try," said Lara.

"And we will," agreed Emily.

Jamie hadn't even moved. He was growing used to Emily's wild ideas. But that didn't mean he had to take them seriously.

"Oh, sure," he cut in scornfully. "You just walk on to the runway and they order all the planes to stop while you wander around looking for foxcubs."

They ignored him. "We'd need a box of some kind, to put them in," said Lara.

"A bag." Emily got to her knees. "A school bag. Then if anyone asks we can say we're on a picnic."

Lara sat up further, growing more excited. "We can take some food for them, too. Chicken or something."

"And some milk." The two girls were wide-eyed with delight as the ideas came tumbling out of them; and with every word Jamie's mouth dropped further and his face grew more alarmed.

"You can't be serious," he gasped. "Look; forget it. Some of those planes are enormous. You'd get flattened. And if you got caught . . . well – they'd probably sling you in jail!"

Harry added: "They're probably dead by now anyway."

Lara snatched up the paper. She pointed to the date line at the bottom. "Friday. That's three days ago. They might be okay. We can't just leave them."

She studied the page. "What was that bit . . . Listen." She quoted from the page. " *'We've searched the north, south and east boundaries* . . .' If they haven't done the west boundary yet, maybe that's where they are. It's a starting point at least."

"It's probably a runway," shrieked Jamie, incredulously. "You just wander all over a runway and they'll shoot you or something . . . or you'll get chopped up by the propellers."

"It's jets nowadays, Jamie dear; they don't have propellers," said Emily sweetly, looking at Lara with a gleam in her eye. "When?"

"Now. Straight away. If they *are* alive they'll be running out of time. We've got all afternoon to get there. And the evening will be a good time to start. That's when foxes are awake, and there won't be so much traffic about."

"We'll get the bus in," said Emily. "We had chicken last night. There might be some left. I'll bring that; and my school bag."

"And mine. We might need more than one."

Jamie shook his head. "You're barmy. You'll never do it. For a start, you've got no idea where to look; and second, they just don't let people wander all over airports."

"But they haven't put up all the fences, yet," said Lara. "And it's not like an international airport, where it has to be secure because of terrorists and things."

Harry asked Lara, "You'll be late back. What about when Mum and Dad notice you're missing?"

The girls were standing up, brushing the grass off their jeans. "Tell them we're over playing at Jamie's house," said Lara. "You can think up something."

"Well I think you're crazy," said Jamie.

"Maybe," agreed Emily happily, "but if we can do it . . . just think: we'd save the poor things from an awful death for a start, and we'd have real wild animals for the zoo. No-one could argue with that." She raised a fist in the air and shouted, "Up your pipe, Sean the brawn!"

"I bet you don't do it," said Harry.

"Okay clever-dick," Lara prodded him in the shoulder, "Here's a deal. If we bring them back, then you've all got to find an animal for the zoo, too. And a real wild animal. Something proper. Not just an ordinary pet."

"Don't be daft, where are we going to find something like that."

"That's your problem. You can buy them, out of your share of the profits."

Harry and Jamie exchanged glances. Jamie nodded, cautiously. "You're off your heads. What if you don't . . . bring them back, that is?"

"Then you get our share." Emily turned to Lara. "All right?"

Lara nodded. "Done."

Ellen wailed. "That's not fair. I'm too little. I can't find a wild animal. And I want to spend my money on sweets. You can't have it. I'm telling Mum."

"Better leave her out of it," said Lara. "She's too small."

Emily placed her hands on Ellen's shoulders and looked earnestly into her face. "Look Ellen. You don't have to join in because you didn't bet. It's just the boys, against us girls. All three of us. If we find any cubs they'll be yours, too. Right?"

Ellen nodded.

"But it has to be a secret. We mustn't tell anyone about this. Do you promise?"

"Course," sniffed Ellen. "I'm not a tell-tale." She looked down her nose at the boys, and stepped over to stand between Emily and Lara. "Us girls against you two," she simpered, triumphantly.

"And just to be sure they don't tell," said Emily, winking at the others. "You'll have to stay with them, and keep an eye on them 'til we get back. Okay?"

"Okay." Ellen fixed the two boys with a sinister gaze.

"Come on," said Lara, pulling at Emily's sleeve. "let's go and get ready."

The real night, deep and thick and close to the window, had arrived by the time Jamie opened the curtains for the tenth time. Still no sign of them.

Emily's mother had been over to insist her daughter went home; and he had blushed and stumbled with a lie: she had gone into the garden to be certain Sounds was properly shut in.

"I don't know why she couldn't have left that rabbit outside the house as it was," her mother said irritably.

Shortly after, he heard Emily's father calling her name into the dark shadows of the thickening twilight.

And then Harry was hammering at the back door. "Where are they?" he hissed intently. "Mum's threatening murder if I don't bring Lara back with me this time. I can't say she's just coming again."

"Who's that, Jamie?" called his mother from within the house.

"Only Harry. He wants to borrow some of my comics." Jamie signalled Harry to come in and ushered him up the stairs. "We won't be long."

"Don't be; it's time you were heading for bed. And don't disturb Ellen. She's already asleep."

Ellen met them at the top of the stairs. Jamie raised his eyebrows with an exasperated sigh, but let her into his bedroom anyway.

And now, for the tenth time, they were peering into the dark, shielding the reflection of the bedroom light against the glass so they could see better.

There was a "thunk" against the pane and all three jumped back in surprise as a tussock of grass scraped down the window, leaving a dirty mark behind it.

Beneath them Emily was waving urgently. Lara stood beside her, a schoolbag clutched under each arm.

Jamie, Harry and Ellen were down the stairs and through the back door in seconds in a hurried, whispering, rush.

"Where have you been—" began Ellen, but Jamie put a hand over her mouth, nodded into the dense dark of the garden, and in a furtive line they melted through the undergrowth.

Jamie led the way to the shed. As the door scraped open he heard the mice in their cage, scurrying out of sight. He felt across the workbench top for a piece of candle and some matches.

A muffled whimper came from one of the bags. Emily's beam of triumph threatened to split her face in two as she and Lara hurriedly struggled with the bag straps and threw back the flaps. They were all silent, staring into the shadowed bags as the dark interiors flicked and dodged with the movement of the candle light. They caught their breath as a nose appeared, and the tips of two pointed ears.

They rose up until the children could see, bright and fearful in the pale, soft fur, a small dark eye. The head turned cautiously and looked at them like a glove puppet on a hidden hand.

Suddenly, from the other bag, a second head, twin of the first, popped up, and the effect was so comical it broke the tension and set them laughing.

"I don't believe it," breathed Jamie. "I didn't think you had a chance."

"Brill-i-ant," expounded Harry emphatically. "Look, they're just the same."

As if to emphasize the fact, one of the cubs scrambled out of its bag and trundled on short, rocky legs over to the other.

"How did you find them?"

Emily was lost in the depths of her broad, delighted grin as she studied the cubs. Lara told the story with relish.

"We nearly didn't. It was absolutely black and we'd given up. We couldn't find our way back. You know those little posts in the ground with lights on top, round the edge of the runway? Well, we just walked from one to the next. I nearly died when a plane went over. I thought it was going to land on us. It was so close! After it had gone we were walking past one of the posts when we heard a noise.

"It was right under our feet! You know around the bottom of posts, how all the tussocky bits of grass grow 'cos you can't get the mower near. Well, that's how it was round these posts. And right up against one of them was a hole. We'd never have found it, but just then another plane shrieked past us. We must've been practically on the runway. As the lights went by we saw all the earth scraped back where the foxes had dug. We pulled the grass back and – there it was!"

Harry was wide-eyed. "How did you get them out?"

"The chicken. We just held it in front of the hole. They must have been starving, poor things. They almost sprinted out. They didn't seem at all frightened. I suppose they haven't learned to be – yet."

"We nearly got caught!" interrupted Emily.

"Maybe they saw us from one of the planes and radioed a message. We stuffed the cubs in the bags and were heading back – not that we had too much idea which way we were supposed to go – when two lights came bouncing across the grass towards us. It was a sort of jeep. Two policemen got out. They were ever so cross. Wanted to know what we were doing there—"

"The cubs kept wriggling," broke in Lara.

Everyone laughed, but Lara went on, "No, it wasn't funny. They never noticed but they might have. We told them we'd gone for a picnic and got lost. We must have looked terrified, because they were quite nice then. Gave us a ride back to the bus stop.

"But we couldn't catch a bus. Not with them." She pointed to the cubs, now peering upside down over the edge of the work bench. "We walked the whole way. We're exhausted."

"You're in trouble," said Jamie. He explained how Emily's parents had been pursuing her with increasing impatience.

"And Mum's pretty hacked off with you." Harry nodded towards Lara.

"We'd better settle this pair down then, and get going," said Lara.

"They need more food," said Emily. "And water. They haven't eaten for three days, don't forget. Except chicken. And there wasn't much of that," she added regretfully.

"It's going to have to be mouse bread tonight, and water," said Jamie. "We can shut them in here."

71

Quickly they shook the insects out of a heap of ancient sacking and piled it in a corner. They lifted the cubs down and placed them gently on it. One waddled off and peed immediately on the bare boards.

They placed the stale bread and a bowl of water in front of the cubs; in seconds they had emptied the water and were speedily reducing the bread to crumbs.

"At least it'll keep them busy for a bit," said Emily. She turned to the others. "Now, first thing tomorrow, we've all got to be up early to see to them properly. Right?

"And . . . uh . . . by the way." She paused. Harry and Jamie looked up. Emily had her arm over Lara's shoulder. The enormous grin was back in place. "We did it," she said. "Lara and me." There was a challenge in her voice. "So now it's up to you two . . ."

Before they could answer there was a wail from Ellen. Her face crumpled and she burst into tears, stamping with impotent fury at the bare boards.

"You said it was us girls against them!" she wept. "All three of us. I knew you were tricking. Just because I'm littlest. You're always leaving me out. You're all horrible and I hate you."

"I meant you, too, of course," said Emily hastily.

Ellen paused to gulp in another vast breath. "No, you didn't. Not then. You let it slip out, and that's what you really think. Well, I don't care. I don't want anything to do with your stupid fox cubs, or your mouldy zoo." She hurled herself at the shed door, bursting it open and throwing herself into the night, her cry fading in the distance as she made her way back to the house.

Emily turned to the others, embarrassed to have been the cause, and concerned at Ellen's distress. "I didn't mean it to sound like that," she said. "It was just a way of speaking . . ."

"She should have been in bed hours ago," said Jamie. "She's just tired. She'll have forgotten about it in the morning."

"Shhh!" Lara held a hand out to silence them, and they listened.

Far off, through the blanket of trees and undergrowth they heard Jamie's mother calling his name.

Another voice began . . . "Emily . . . Emily!"

Emily blew out the candle and the four of them filed through the door, tugging it shut behind them and fixing it closed with a bent nail in the hasp catch.

Six

Ellen had not forgotten next morning. They cajoled and coaxed and wheedled and she absorbed it all with imperious disdain. She remained stretched face-down on her bed, reading, kicking her heels in casual unconcern while first Emily, then Lara, then Harry had grovelled at the door for her to come and join them. Only Jamie would have nothing to do with it.

"You must be nuts," he said. "She's loving it. She can keep this up for days. I've got better things to do."

He left them putting the finishing touches to a makeshift kennel and run for the fox cubs.

A short time after, he returned for a spade. His face was flushed and his hands were covered in dirt. They asked what he was doing, but he shrugged off the question and was gone.

It was early afternoon before he came back, carrying a hessian sack, a glow on his dirt-streaked cheeks and the light of triumph in his eyes.

He placed the sack carefully on the ground in front of them and beamed in spite of himself.

Emily studied the sack quizzically. She looked at Jamie, wrinkling her nose. "What is it?"

Before he could answer Lara gave a shriek and stepped back a pace. "It moved! I saw it move. He's got something alive in there."

Jamie's beam became a huge, flushed grin. He crouched to untie the neck of the sack and the others drew forward; three heads watched intently, hardly breathing.

Jamie opened up the neck, peering into its dark interior. He reached confidently into the opening with one hand.

He carefully withdrew it, exposing to view in his firm grasp a blunt nose and two unwinking eyes in a pale green head; a reptilian head, plated and bright. As he drew it out a long body uncoiled endlessly. It wound and writhed in a rope of gloss that was vivid green along its back and creamy white on the belly.

Jamie reached down and gathered up the coils with his other hand, until the whole creature was out of the sack, staring inscrutably into the sunlight. Its triangular head peered out from one side of Jamie's grasp; its body was a writhing green rope that sought to gain a purchase on his arm.

He was breathless with pride. "It's a grass snake," he said. "Look at it. It must be over a metre long."

They were rivetted, open-mouthed.

"Wow!" breathed Harry.

"It's so beautiful," said Lara.

Emily shuddered, involuntarily. "God, I hate snakes," she muttered. "I hate them. Urgh!"

Lara moved forward, entranced, and reached out a hand. "Where did you find it?"

"I didn't think about it until you made the bet about the cubs," said Jamie. "But I saw it last year, on a compost heap Mum started.

"I got the job of taking the potato peelings and things to chuck on it and one day I saw this grass snake slither away.

"They like compost heaps; so I thought it might have hung around. The compost heap was all overgrown with grass and weeds and some of the peelings had sprouted into potato plants. I pulled one aside and – there it was. I don't know who got the biggest shock.

"Anyway it slithered under an old piece of corrugated iron before I could grab it. The weeds had grown over it and I couldn't lift it out. That's why I came back for the spade." His eyes shone with pride.

Lara reached out and touched the snake's skin. "It's so dry," she said, surprised. "I expected it to be slimy. Emily, have a feel; it's amazing."

Emily's face had collapsed to a mixture of fear and revulsion. "No chance," she said. "I can't stand snakes."

"But it's harmless," Lara insisted.

Emily shook her head. "Look, it's brilliant. I'm really impressed, Jamie. But if that thing ever comes near me I'm going to drop dead, I promise. I can't stand 'em. And if my mum ever sees it she'll go through this lot . . ." she indicated the overgrown garden ". . . with a bulldozer. She's terrified. It'll be great for the zoo, but please – please – keep it away from me."

Jamie turned to Harry. "This is my contribution." He held the snake aloft. "Now it's your turn."

Harry grinned and winked. "Don't you worry about me. I've got something in mind."

Next day they found an aquarium big enough for the snake at a local junk yard. The glass on one side had been smashed, but they manhandled it home between them, cleared out all the broken shards and replaced it with a sheet of thin plywood. They banged some breathing holes in another sheet which they used for a roof.

"You'll have to do the rest yourself," said Harry, levering himself from the floor where he had been struggling to fit the plywood in place. "I've got to see someone."

It was three hours before he returned. The two older girls were with Jamie, peering in at the snake. A painted sign on the glass said:

Vivarium (reptile house).

There was no sign of Ellen who still doggedly refused to have anything to do with them.

They were so intent on the snake they failed to hear Harry's approach. He gave a heavy stage sigh of exhaustion and they looked up. He stood behind them, his forehead misted with a fine perspiration. Gripped in both hands he held a bell-like structure covered in a loose cloth. It was nearly as tall as Harry as he struggled to hold its weight clear of the ground.

"This is my part of the bet," he gasped, gently placing his burden on the ground.

They were all on their feet, circling it curiously.

"Any guesses?" grinned Harry.

They shrugged and shook their heads. "A two-ton canary?" offered Emily.

"Close, but not quite. I just grip the cloth here and . . . hey presto!" Harry flicked the material aside to reveal, as Emily had suspected, a cage. It was a huge cage, made not of wire, but of cane, with ornate curling patterns woven into its sides. It formed a cylinder, flat at the bottom, curving together at the top where the cane had been woven to form the handle.

It was indeed big enough for a two-ton canary; but sitting instead in lonely splendour on a wooden perch in the centre was a small and uninspiring bird.

It was mostly black, and little bigger than a starling. Its only distinguishing features were its orange beak and a small yellow flash behind each eye. It cocked an eye at the group, watching them suspiciously. They watched it back, disappointed.

Harry sensed their opinion. "It's a mynah bird," he explained brightly. "It talks; really well."

"It looks a bit like a starling," offered Lara suspiciously.

"Have you *heard* it talk?" said Emily in the same tone.

"No, but the guy in the pub—"

"Pub?" put in Jamie.

Harry began from the beginning. "It was advertised

78

in the paper. That one you were reading the other day. So I rang up. He said it really talks well, but apparently they're ever so messy. It throws water and food all over the place and his wife wouldn't let him keep it."

Harry thrust out his chin with pride. "He wanted ten pounds, but I knocked him down to a fiver."

Emily clapped a hand to her forehead, Jamie shook his head quietly and Lara gasped, "A fiver!"

Harry nodded. He was getting irritated by their tone. "It's out of my share," he snapped. "What's it to you!"

Lara slapped her hands against her sides in a gesture of helplessness. "Couldn't we have got hold of a starling, maybe, and painted its beak orange? It would have been cheaper."

"But it talks!" insisted Harry, hotly.

Jamie asked: "Did he tell you what it said? Maybe we can try a few things."

They looked at the bird. Emily leaned down and said to it, "Hello . . . hello. Who's a pretty boy, then . .?"

Nothing happened.

She glanced up at Harry. "What do we try now? A rock song?"

"Give it a chance. It's probably terrified of your great gawking gob shouting through the bars." Harry's mood was deteriorating fast as his punctured pride deflated.

They all looked at each other. "Maybe we could offer a prize for the first person to get it to say something," offered Lara.

The four of them were turning the idea over in their minds, staring blankly into the cage when, without warning, the bird said, "Hellooo."

They looked at each other, mouths open. "Looks like he was right—" began Jamie. The bird took over with a sudden burst, "Hellooo; hello; hello; hellooo."

The children grinned. Emily clapped Harry on the back and a broad, happy smile blossomed on his face. The bird cut in again.

"Hellooo . . . ratbag!"

Harry's mouth hung open. His eyes popped; Emily's, Lara's and Jamie's too. They turned purple and exploded into laughter. Jamie fell over, slapping his thigh and gasping.

The bird carried on through the hysteria in an elderly man's voice: "Ratbag. Old ratbag. Shuddup ratbag. Hellooo."

Emily snorted through her closed mouth, tears streaming down her face. Lara clung to her shoulder, her other hand clapped over one ear, gasping for breath. "No—, no wonder— he wanted—, wanted to get rid of it," she snorted.

The bird had subsided into silence, beaking its ruffled feathers.

Jamie propped himself on an elbow on the grass and spluttered: "It— it must've been the— the customers who taught him."

The others were weak and tearful with delight. There was a short silence, broken by the clear tones of the mynah bird, this time in a perfect cockney accent: "you old b—."

The final word was drowned as the four of them fell back, shrieking with laughter that hurt their faces and made their chests ache.

Emily recovered enough to splutter, "Harry, it's a winner. I'm sorry I was so rude about it."

They all lay back with tears of pleasure threading down from the corners of their eyes and their chests pumping. There was a slight movement in the bushes and a voice snorted: "I don't know what's so funny, but I can hear you back at the house."

Lara looked up: "Ellen! It's Ellen." She was on her feet in a moment. "Come and look at this Ellen."

She led the little girl to the cage. "It's a mynah bird. It talks." She waited, but the bird said nothing.

"Hello; hello; hellooo," prompted Lara. Ellen watched, unmoved as a brick. The bird swivelled its head and picked at a feather on its back, saying nothing.

"Looks like a starling," said Ellen with a superior sniff.

"It really does talk," said Harry, giggling. "And it's a bit rude. It hasn't got a name. You can choose one, if you like."

Ellen stared at them. "You're all so childish."

Emily knelt down in front of her. "Please Ellen," she pleaded. "I know this is all my fault; and I *am* sorry. Come and join us. It doesn't seem . . . well, the same, without you."

"No thank you. I shan't play until I've got an animal, too." Her lower lip began to wobble.

Jamie snorted. "I can't stand this. She's enjoying it."

Emily stopped him. "Jamie; it's not very nice to feel left out."

"Oh come on, Emily. She's five years old and if you must know I'm sick of dragging her around with me. If she wants to sulk all day that's fine by me."

Colour rose up Ellen's neck and into her face. Her lower lip stopped wobbling and her whole mouth set in a grim line as the flush of red swept up into her hair.

Her eyes narrowed and she spat out, "It's not much fun being with you either!" She turned on her heel and marched into the undergrowth. The bushes closed around her and she was gone.

"You're a bit tough on her," said Lara mildly. "She's only small."

"Oh, don't give me that," snapped Jamie. "You know what she's like. You've known her long enough."

"Some brother," murmured Emily.

He blazed at her. "You keep out of it. I get her every day while Mum's at work and I don't have to put up with you, too. Just keep out of it or push off!"

"I'm sorry. I didn't realize – about your mum!" she shouted back. "You can leave her with us if you like and push off yourself if it's that much of a drag!"

"Aagh. You'd probably lose her or something."

"Well; surprise, surprise. He cares! I thought you'd be delighted."

Fuming, he ignored her and turned to study the

mynah bird. Emily's eyes burned angrily into his back. "Don't worry yourself about it. *I'll* see if she's okay." There was no response, so she went after Ellen, through the bushes to home. Lara went with her.

"He's very fond of her really, you know," said Lara, as she hurried along beside Emily.

"Of course he is. I've made a long list of all the nice things he's said about her," snapped Emily sarcastically. "Nothing; never. Zero; not once."

"But you saw how he protected her when Sean was bullying; and you, if it comes to that."

The words struck home, evaporating Emily's anger. The menace of Sean was still fresh in her mind; so was her relief when Jamie arrived to help. She slowed down, turning to Lara. "Then why is he so . . . surly, sometimes?"

Lara shrugged. "I'm not sure. He's shy, I know that. He never says a word to my parents. They think he's surly, too."

"Hmm; they're not wrong, either."

"Get to know him better," urged Lara. "He likes you a lot. Just don't expect him to show it, that's all."

Emily slapped her hands against her thighs in frustration. "And what use is it if he doesn't show it? Big deal."

"Please?" Lara persisted.

Emily sighed heavily, mouth set, not looking up.

They found Ellen in her bedroom lying on her stomach, her feet banging angrily down on to the covers. She was drawing in crayon on a pad of paper.

The picture was a wild-eyed, monstrous black creature with scribbled hair and teeth like knives. Underneath Ellen had written: J-A-M-E-E. "Go away," she said. "I don't want to join in. Go away."

"If we can find you an animal of your own, would that help?"

Ellen shook her head.

"Well, what can we do."

"Nothing. Go away." She was scrubbing out her brother's picture with a red crayon. Lara and Emily walked away with a sigh, closing the door behind them.

Seven

Ellen woke next morning with sun knifing through her window blinds. A sense of desolation consumed her. She couldn't go back now. She had sulked too long to go back. They wouldn't *say* anything if she did, but it would be understood that she had given in.

So she wasn't going back unless she had an animal of her own. It didn't have to be much; Harry's was just a scruffy old bird in a cage. The cage was better than the bird. *They* said it talked, but she hadn't heard it.

She needed an animal, anything; and she could go back triumphant. It was all right for them. They could go off exploring the airport, and buying stuff. But she couldn't do that without them, and she couldn't – wouldn't! – ask.

Whatever she found, it had to be in the garden. Even some frogspawn would be better than nothing. She remembered once seeing a lizard on the wall. A shudder scrambled up her spine. Yuk! It would mean picking it up. Maybe she could trap it with a plastic bowl.

She sneaked a bowl from her mother's cupboard

and headed for the garden. She kept well away from where they were setting up the zoo. Following one of the narrow tracks through the undergrowth she found a flat rock, which she gingerly turned over with her foot. She backed away pulling a face when woodlice and ants scattered from under it. A slug squirmed darkly. She found an old rusty tin and peered in, but it was full only of foul-smelling water. She pulled another face.

She did find a lizard. She rolled a dead branch aside and it was startled to stillness for a brief moment before it scuttled into the undergrowth. She stamped her foot, cross with herself for not being ready.

There was a crashing of branches ahead and the unmistakeable sound of Scab's voice as he barged through the undergrowth. Other cats only miaowed; Scab sounded like gravel under a heavy boot.

She called to him, "Sca-ab, Scabby, Scabby Scab." The cat appeared further up the narrow track, padding lightly towards her.

He stopped and peered at her, winking one scarred eye. She coaxed him forward, but he wouldn't respond. With a little "tch" of irritation she walked towards him and the cat turned with its kinked tail in the air and walked away.

She knew Scab would make the perfect hunter. If she could persuade him, he would catch whatever they unearthed. No lizard would get away from Scab. Not even a mouse. Not even a rat! "No, not a rat," she thought, shuddering. "I can't handle a rat."

Scab jumped off the track and disappeared from view. She reached the place where he had gone. It was no more than a hole in the undergrowth; she bent double and followed, still calling.

The bushes opened into a little glade, heavily shadowed, with leaves of sunlight sprinkled over it. She heard Scab's gravel-miaow before she saw him. He was nestled at the foot of a great dark boulder, or maybe an old, smoothed tree stump. It was hard to tell in the half-light..

She stepped forward. In the warm summer air and soft shadows, Scab curled peacefully. The glade was thick with tranquillity. She could hear Scab purring; and another sound . . . like Scab's, but deeper, soaking through her and round her.

Ellen squinted in the half-light. The boulder, it was coming from the boulder: or was it a tree stump? As she watched, the shape stirred gently; the faintest movement, that you might feel you had not really seen – then it raised its head.

Ellen gave a little jump of surprise. The head was as big as her own, and two yellow eyes burned out of it, studied Ellen, and vanished as the lids fell sleepily over them; then they reappeared.

She moved forward again, and the shape transformed itself into mounded folds of fur that swept in graceful curves up to sinuous shoulders and an arched neck, topped by a sleek cat head.

It was purring. That was the sound she could hear. Scab, nestled between the creature's forepaws, knew how to purr. His was long and deep and vibrant; but this sound drowned even Scab's purr. It was more intense, deeper and harder; like a distant earthquake. The sound felt as if it was vibrating up through the soles of Ellen's feet.

The creature was lying down and partly shadowed; so although she could see it was enormous she had no idea how big, nor would she have until it stood up.

Unaware of what she faced, Ellen stepped up to it. "Puss, puss," she called. "Scab, you've got a friend." The buzz of contentment from the two cats grew louder. The moulded, flowing shape of the big cat was dark as sleep, shadow on shadow, mysterious. But in essential details it looked like Scab. Much bigger, more elegant, less battle-scarred; but a cat nonetheless.

"Here pussy; puss, puss." She reached out a hand and buried it in the deep, black gloss of the warm fur.

An older child might have known enough to be frightened; but Ellen felt only the warm glow of discovery, and a gentle desire for comfort, such as she felt when she pillowed into her mother's lap.

"Aren't you big!" she breathed, and slid her arm sideways over the dark, deep fur of the animal's neck. She hugged herself into it. Scab came purring to join her, climbing fearlessly up the panther's foreleg, kneading its shoulder with his claws.

For many minutes Ellen lay cradled in the warm luxury and hypnotic tone of the continuous purr. She was sprawled entirely over the animal, her feet clear of the ground. "You can be my cat," she whispered. "I bet you're the biggest cat in the world. And the beautifulest." She looked from it to

88

Scab. "We've got the beautifulest and the ugliest. Wait 'til the others see."

The others. She thought for a moment, then slid off the panther's sweeping back and with one hand scratching at its ear, she looked at its elegant head, thinking.

"You've got to come with me," she said, looking down the creature's length. "I can't carry you." She

gripped tentatively a handful of neck fur. "Come on." She tugged. The panther scowled a cat-scowl, opening its mouth and drawing back its lips to show its huge, curved fangs.

Ellen was unperturbed. She looked down at Scab. "You look after him, Scab. All right? Don't let him go anywhere. I'll bring a tin of your sardines. You don't mind sharing, do you?"

Scab was busy burying his head in the panther's flank.

"Wait there," she called. "I won't be long." She edged her way to the side of the glade, urging them to wait, until they were out of her sight.

She saw the panther make a silent "miaow" as she dropped the screen of bushes into place. She hurtled down the path, careering past branches that lashed at her cheeks, stumbling over rocks, her breath coming harder and harder until she burst, panting, into the clearing where the others were preparing the zoo. The sound of her crashing through the undergrowth had preceded her and they were all staring in her direction.

"Hello," said Lara with relief. "We thought you might be Sean again. Have you come to help?"

Ellen shot past without speaking, heading for the shed. The others hurried after. They reached her as she climbed down from the workbench. A tin of Scab's catfood was in her hand.

"What on earth are you doing now?" grumbled Jamie. Lara placed a restraining hand on his arm. Emily withered him with a look. "You're busy," she said brightly. "What's the problem?"

Ellen looked at them all. "I've got my own animal," she said smugly.

Lara clapped her hands. "Great," she offered. "What is it?" She really sounded interested and Ellen warmed to her tone.

"It's a cat." She glanced around them as they looked at one another. Jamie's eyes flicked skywards and the corners of his mouth turned down.

"We've got a cat," he breathed.

Emily scowled at him forcefully. "We can have two cats," she said turning to Ellen. "It doesn't matter. Where is it?"

Ellen became agitated. "I've got to hurry. It might go away. Scab's looking after it."

Jamie laughed harshly. "Huh, looking after it. He's probably eaten it."

"I don't think so. It's bigger than Scab."

The others exchanged disbelieving glances. There was a pause and Emily said: "Nothing's bigger than Scab. Not cats anyway. It isn't possible."

"Most *dogs* are smaller than Scab," agreed Harry.

Jamie moaned, "Oh look, this is a waste of time. We've got one ca- ouch!"

Lara silenced him with an elbow in the ribs. "Shut up," she whispered from the corner of her mouth. "if it keeps her happy, that's fine. Come on, then," she said to Ellen. "Better lead us to it."

"Better take this, then," said Jamie with a sigh. He handed a tin opener to Ellen.

"Thanks," she said and shot off. The others tried hard to retain their dignity by striding after her, instead of running. Feather gambolled along behind, panting. When they were near the spot Ellen stopped. "Now; it only knows me, so you mustn't frighten it. I'll go first and you all stay back 'til I say it's all right. It's mine, don't forget. So you all have to do what I say."

Jamie groaned. "This is great. She's really putting the boot in."

Harry shrugged. "Who cares. It'll keep her happy; stop her being a pain. Smile; it'll soon be over."

"You'll have to hold Feather," she ordered. "It might be frightened."

"I'm smiling," growled Jamie quietly as he held Feather's collar. "I'm smiling."

They followed on Ellen's heels as she disappeared into the glade.

As their eyes adjusted to the reduced light, they saw the dark shape of the boulder; was it a boulder? Or a tree stump? A small shape detached itself and proudly stalked towards them, tail in the air.

"That's Scab," said Emily. "Wotcha Scab, I wondered where you'd got to."

"Well, where's Ellen's cat?" asked Harry. They peered.

Ellen was leaning against the boulder. They were aware of the deep vibration in the air. A wind caught in the high trees and swept back the branches, admitting a cone of light that spread over the glade, slid over the boulder. Quick as a fingersnap it was a boulder no longer. The head lifted, sunlight glinted off the yellow eyes, and the yellow eyes glinted into those of Harry, Emily, Lara and Jamie.

The deep fur rippled across its shoulders as Ellen ran her fingers through it. The panther opened its mouth in a silent miaow, for all the world like an angry spitting.

"Erk," gurgled Jamie.

"Eeek," squeaked Harry.

"Oh my God," gasped Lara.

Emily made an indescribable noise in her throat

and gripped Jamie's arm hard with both hands while she sidled round behind him. He didn't feel the pain as her nails dug in.

Feather whimpered and lay down with his head low in the long grass trying to pretend he wasn't there.

The big cat leaned its head, putting Ellen's hand in the vicinity of its ear and squinted with pleasure as she scratched behind it.

"It's . . ." croaked Jamie.

Emily nodded.

Harry backed away carefully. "I'll go and get help." He squeaked.

"No! No, not yet. We must get Ellen away," said Lara. "Now Ellen; just listen, Ellen. You'll be all right if you don't make any sudden movements."

Her stomach quaked, but she took a deep breath and went on, "I want you to stand up slowly and walk over here to me. Don't run, whatever you do."

Ellen's mouth dropped open as she sat up in the seat she had made for herself in the curve of the animal's side. "What *are* you talking about?"

Emily's voice bubbled into action. "It's not a cat, you idiot. It's a panther. It must be that panther in the newspaper. It's dangerous. Look at it. Look at the size of it!"

"It is big, isn't it," agreed Ellen proudly. "But it's not dangerous." She was struggling with the tin as she spoke. "I can't open this thing." She held the tin and opener out to the others. "Jamie, will you do it for me. Please."

"Who . . . er . . . me?" he quaked.

93

Ellen nodded.

Jamie held his hand out. "Bring it here then."

Ellen sat and watched them all for a moment. Their fear was transmitted to her just as the panther's purr transmitted its tranquillity. The tremble in their voices was like a window to their thoughts.

Ellen narrowed her eyes. "No," she grinned wickedly. "You come here. Unless you're frightened . . ."

Jamie's knees made walking movements, but his feet didn't go anywhere. He became aware vaguely of Emily's nails digging into his arm. He prised her off. "It doesn't seem to mind Ellen."

"No," agreed Emily, stepping back.

"And she *is* my sister. If I can get her away . . ."

Emily nodded.

He wiped his forehead. His feet began to move. Scab padded ahead of him, kinked tail erect, giving him courage. The others stood and watched, sweat beading on their faces. Feather whimpered, belly to the ground, behind Harry.

As Jamie approached, the resonant purr grew louder. It occurred to him that if a cat was purring it could hardly be dangerous. But then again, he had heard Scab purr while he ate a grasshopper.

He stretched out to take the can and opener from Ellen. He applied the opener and as it popped through the metal the smell of jellied sardines rose into Jamie's face, oily strong.

The panther smelled it, too, and lifted its head. Jamie, startled, nearly dropped the can. Gradually he wound the opener round the lid. It dropped noiselessly to the grass. Scab was standing on his hindlegs with a forepaw on Jamie's knee, yowling hungrily. The panther raised itself up on its forelegs and Ellen slid out of her seat in its fur.

Then it stood up. Gently it eased itself from the ground until it stood taller than Ellen. Its tail looped down, clearing the ground in an elegant curve. The shimmering light through the trees marked the beauty of its muscled body in shadowed relief. The gloss of its black fur mirrored the sunlight in the gloom.

While Jamie clutched the tin to his chest, the panther put its nose in it. Jamie nearly fainted.

He might have done, too, if it hadn't been for the squeal of horror from Emily. He looked up and saw them all backing into the bushes as the big cat moved. Trembling, he dropped the tin which hit the grass on its side. Scab was on it like a drowning man.

Something brushed Jamie's leg. He looked down as the velvet body of the panther sidled noiselessly round him. Its head went down, heading for the tin. Scab's growling reached earthquake proportions, but it didn't stop the panther nudging him aside. It sniffed at the tin. A large pink tongue, rough as gravel, slid out and licked at the surface of the jellied contents. The animal poked at the tin with a paw, but it rolled away, towards Jamie's foot. He was transfixed, eyes boggling. Only Ellen moved. "You silly old thing," she tutted. "We'll have to get it out first." She armed herself with a stick and moved forward. Bending, she snatched the tin from under the panther's nose. There was a groan of despair from the group by the bushes.

Ellen peered into the tin. Beside her, ear to ear, the panther peered in, too. Ellen slid the stick in, upended the tin and pulled. The contents flopped out on to the grass with a squelch and the panther was on them. Scab contented himself with the empty tin.

The sardines vanished off the grass in two mouthfuls. The panther spent a little more time sniffing out the odd flakes stuck to blades of grass before he raised his head to Ellen. He purred deeply as his tongue came out and he licked fishily at her cheek. "Ouch!" she squealed. "That's rough."

The panther nosed into her hands like a horse looking for sugar lumps. Ellen spread her open palms. "It's all gone. There isn't any more. Not here, anyway."

The panther padded to where Jamie stood, limp as a wet dishrag, and nosed into his hands, too. A plaintive squeak gurgled from Jamie's throat, but the only part of him that moved was the thumping pulse in his temple.

Harry bit hard on his fingers; Emily and Lara clung to each other, eyes wide, breath held. The panther's rough, pink tongue explored Jamie's trembling fingers, found nothing, and the animal returned its attention to the grass.

"It seems okay," whispered Lara. "I can't believe it."

Emily nodded.

"Are you all right, Jamie?" called Harry through his fingers.

"Do I look all right?" wheezed Jamie. "Get my mum. Get the police."

Ellen, who had been picking up the empty tin, whirled round. "You can't do that. I found him and he's going to be in our zoo."

Lara had unlocked herself from Emily's grasp and was edging forward nervously. "You don't think you can keep it, do you? It's a wild animal. I mean, really wild. You've read about them in books. They eat . . . well—"

"Customers?" volunteered Harry.

"And you need a licence," added Emily.

Ellen's mouth set in an angry line. She placed her hands on her hips and stamped. "Just 'cos I got a better animal than all you!" she blazed.

The panther dismissed Jamie's hand and turned its attention to Scab who was rubbing around its front leg.

"It didn't touch me," breathed Jamie incredulously. "I'm still here." He held his hand in front of his face, to prove it was true.

Harry sidled slowly back toward the bushes. "I'll go and get someone," he whispered.

"No!" shouted Ellen. She flung her arms suddenly round the panther's neck. The rapid movement made it leap back, silently showing its teeth. Ellen was still locked round its neck, but the others froze instantly, terror shaping their faces.

"I *won't* give him up. He wouldn't hurt a fly." Before Jamie had time to think she grabbed his hand and pushed it deep in the panther's fur. "See?" she said. "See? You're so stupid. He's just a big pussy cat. He's purring. Can't you hear? It's like an engine."

Lara and Emily looked at Jamie. He hadn't taken his hand out of the fur. He shook his head, unbelievingly. "It seems okay," he said simply. "It, er– it really seems to be enjoying it."

Even Harry had taken a few steps forward.

Ellen took the initiative. She kissed the side of the creature's head. It squinted pleasurably and the purr deepened.

"Come on," she coaxed the others. "It's all right, really." She pointed to Scab, who was twining himself in and out of the panther's legs. "Look, Emily; even Scab likes him."

Emily and Lara moved closer, so they could reach the panther by stretching out their hands. They did so. The purring intensified. They looked at each other and grinned. They looked at Jamie and the three of them laughed sheepishly together. Harry, too, had closed in on the group. He reached through and pushed his fingers into the coat. Only Feather hadn't moved, except for an occasional fidget and whimper.

"I don't believe it," whispered Harry.

"Told you," said Ellen, smugly.

Lara said, "Maybe we could keep it, for a while anyway." Her eyes shone. "Wouldn't it be great!"

"I'm keeping it forever and ever," said Ellen firmly.

The warm, deep fur and the constant purring continued to transmit its hypnotic peacefulness to them.

"Oh Boy," said Harry. "Our own panther."

"You got a mynah bird," Ellen reminded him. "This is *my* panther."

"How are we ever going to keep this secret?" said Jamie. "Anyone who comes to the zoo might tell. And there are people out looking for it."

Emily raised a finger dramatically. "We'll make everyone take a solemn oath. And anyway, what would your mum say if you came home and said you'd just seen a panther in someone's garden."

Jamie shrugged. He couldn't deny that no-one would believe it. He hardly believed it himself.

Emily turned to Ellen. "What's his name. You have to give him a name."

Ellen puffed with pride. She beamed into the slotted yellow of the panther's contented eyes; surveyed it from dark tail to velvet black nose-tip. "Blackie," she said triumphantly. She leaned into the animal, crooning, "You're Blackie, aren't you? Blackie . . . Blackie, Blackie. Hello Blackie."

Jamie groaned. "Oh, very original!"

Emily grinned at him. "Oh, don't be such a pain. She did find it, after all. And who cares about the name." She thumped him almost affectionately on the shoulder, and nudged Lara and Harry. "This is the real thing. What a chance; a miracle! No-one can argue with a panther – even one called Blackie. This is real wildlife stuff. I can't wait to see brawny Sean's face!"

Jamie's face dropped. "Hang on . . . he's one person that mustn't find out – ever."

"Why not? I really want to rub his nose in it."

"Look dum-dum," insisted Jamie, "he's the one person who *will* blab; and people *will* listen to him. The garden would be full of police in two minutes. And if it is the one from the paper – and it *must* be, mustn't it? – then it'll end up dead. The judge said it should be put down . . . remember?"

"He's right," agreed Lara.

Emily's face was briefly downcast before it lit up again. "Huh, who cares about him," she breezed. She clapped Ellen on the back. "You stuffed the lot of us." She turned to the panther, who was patting Scab's head with a gentle paw. "This is too much. It's unbelievable."

Harry was on his haunches facing Blackie, eye to eye. "I tell you one thing – if it's the one from the paper it's not a he; it's a she. I remember you reading it out. And that's probably why Scab gets on with it so well; him being a tomcat.

"And another thing – there's no way we're going to feed this one on a few chicken scraps pinched from the fridge. A few chickens, maybe; daily. But this is a serious eating machine we're talking about. Where are we going to get that kind of stuff from?"

Lara said, "We've got a few tins of sardines left. Scab won't mind; we can replace them as soon as we've got some money from customers. He generally catches his own food at night, anyway. But we've got to get him – sorry her, Blackie – back to the shed. She seems fond of Scab; so if you, Emily, pick up Scab (you're the only one who can) maybe she'll follow you. If not, perhaps we can coax her with some more sardines.

"I guess we'll have to beg some bones off the butcher sooner or later. I mean, wild panthers live in jungles; I bet they don't catch fish . . . do they?"

Everyone shrugged, blankly.

"We'll have to keep her in the shed while we work something out. We don't want all the other exhibits ending up inside this one before breakfast."

Eight

By the end of the afternoon they'd made a home for Blackie in the garden shed. They ransacked their own homes for old pillows and worn-out sheets which they piled up as a nest on which the panther could sleep. The mouse cage was moved to a high shelf. Harry ran to the shops and bought a padlock for the door. They couldn't trust a bent nail anymore.

Ellen reluctantly agreed to Blackie being tied on a long rope during the day.

"To stop her wandering off; she might not come back," said Emily.

Lara and Emily sweated away most of the afternoon hacking out a new small, clear area, shielded from curious eyes, which was to be Blackie's run.

They painted a special sign to go at the roadside:

THE NEW WILDLIFE PARK
(round the back)
MORE, BETTER EXOTIC CREATURES.
SEE OUR SECRET WILD ANIMAL
(you will be amazed)

Ellen crept back when no one was looking and changed it to "See Ellen's Secret Wild Animal."

By evening Blackie had finished eleven tins of jellied sardines and half a packet of frankfurters Harry discovered at the back of his parents' refrigerator. Long into the evening, by candlelight, they lay flopped around the panther, too excited to leave; still barely believing this great soft, deadly, awesome creature was in their midst; all except Ellen who thought it wonderful but quite unsurprising.

Before they split up for the night they tipped their money from the tin. There was hardly a handful of change.

"They'd better come," said Lara, "or we won't have enough left to feed the gold fish."

They left Blackie that night curled on her nest of old fabric, her yellow eyes luminous in the twilight, with Scab lying inside the curve of her flank, purring deeply.

Next morning was chaos. Their paths tangled like spilled wool as they hurried on their tasks: feeding and watering animals, setting each one out in its pen, or cage or hutch; changing bedding.

Feather was promoted to guard dog in case Sean returned. The dog nosed under arms, licked faces and generally got in the way – until Ellen proudly led Blackie out, accompanied by Scab fawning at the panther's feet. Feather put his tail down and skulked behind Jamie.

Blackie was secured on a long rope at one side of

her new clearing. Visitors were to be restricted to the far side of the clearing, for safety.

"He's like a kitten," said Lara as the panther butted her affectionately in its search for a scratch behind the ears. "But we'd better not risk it. Anyway; it'll be more exciting if they think it's dangerous."

They agreed to leave Scab with Blackie for company. The two clearly enjoyed being together "and *no-one* but us is going to go near Blackie while Scab's around," Harry predicted.

By lunchtime they were ready.

"I've got the importantest animal," pouted Ellen indignantly. "I don't see why I should stand on the gate all day."

They took turns; Emily agreed to be first. The new sign was doing its work. The queue had already begun by the time she opened the gate. Word spread quickly. By lunchtime children of all ages were filing in. Pretty soon the depleted contents of the tin began to take on some of their former weightiness.

This time there was no doubt – the zoo was a brilliant success. Children studied the beady, black-eyed Dracula in silent suspicion; they squirmed and squealed at the writhing, slit-mouthed, round-eyed grass snake; and they oohed and aahed over the clumsy, gambolling foxcubs.

The mynah bird cage was hung from a tree-branch where children ringed it in disbelieving quiet while Harry coaxed it into voicing yet greater vulgarities. At each one the crowd fell helplessly to the ground, hysterical with laughter.

They grimaced as the braver ones dropped slugs to Cuddles, who now stood his ground and devoured them with chop-smacking pleasure as they fell. They held Sounds and the guinea-pig tenderly in their arms under the solicitous care of Lara who, in Emily's absence at the gate, showed how to carry them. Lara also moved with little groups from creature to creature explaining why it was that mice needed something hard to chew; how snakes shed their skin; where mynah birds came from.

And further off, outside Blackie's clearing, beside a sign proclaiming: "Mystery Animal (Dangerous) do not enter", Jamie and Ellen stood before a solemn crowd, right hands held aloft. They all mumbled a terrible oath that if they ever told a living soul of what they were about to see their eyes would drop out and their tongues would swell and choke them to silence.

Ellen moved aside the curtain of branches and led the group in. The tension in their held breath was audible as they trod the silent clearing, uncertain what shape the mystery would take.

First – as the others had done – they saw the grim-lipped, battered face of Scab. And when the shape behind Scab flicked its black rope of tail and turned its elegant, sculpted face towards them, still they did not understand. Some thought it was a dog; others a trick of the shadows; a tree or a bush maybe.

But as their eyes grew accustomed to the softer light, chins dropped, hands flew to gaping mouths, eyes popped like button mushrooms. Blackie lazily opened yellow eyes and studied the crowd. The light glinted with a crystal gleam off the black gloss of her coat.

She made no other move but to open her jaws and mouth the silent miaow that looked so much like a snarl. The audience gasped and a small boy grabbed Jamie's hand and moved behind him.

"It's all right," bossed Ellen. "She's tied up. She can't get near you. And even if she could she wouldn't hurt you. She's mine you know."

Then Blackie rose. Slowly, loosely she lifted herself from the floor. She slinked a few paces forward. A giant, rumbling purr broke from her throat, travelling through the air and ground, reaching up through the soles of their feet.

They fled.

"Stop!" yelled Jamie. "She won't hurt you. Look." Desperately, before they had gone forever to spread irreparable terror, he grabbed Ellen and ran across to Blackie. They both put their arms round her neck. "Look," he yelled. "She's fine."

A child looked back, and stopped. The ones behind stopped in their flight, and looked back, too. The ones ahead became aware there was no-one following them, and they crept back to see. Blackie turned her head and licked Jamie's hand.

"Can we stroke it?" asked a child.

"No."

"Why not? You are."

"Look. This is a panther, see? It's a wild animal. It eats things. Like children. So just stay there."

"It's not eating her." Someone pointed at Ellen.

A familiar voice cut in: "Oh, I don't know. It should be safe enough." Emily walked across the clearing and whispered to Jamie, "I've got an idea. Just take Blackie to the end of the rope and let them have a quick stroke."

"But . . . "

"Go on. She can't do any harm as long as she's still tied – even if she wanted to. Listen to that purr; she's softer than you are."

Jamie glowered at Emily. He walked gently forward and Blackie padded alongside him, eyes mere lazy slits. The children backed away a little, until finally the rope hung in a long arc off the ground. They eased forward and one by one sank their hands in the creature's polished fur. Their eyes shone. A small child blurted happily, "I'm stroking it! I'm stroking a real live panther."

"How would you like to feed her, too?" said Emily.

Every voice clamoured to be first.

"Right. No problem. But you have to bring the food. She likes cat food. You know, tins. So if you come back with a tin of cat food – sardines in jelly is best – you can feed her. But don't tell anyone . . . "

They were gone, leaving Jamie, Emily and Ellen alone with Scab and Blackie. Emily bent down and scooped Scab from the grass. "So now we don't have to worry about food, either," she said, grinning up at Jamie. "They'll provide it for us." She turned Scab until she was looking into his scarred face. "And there might even be some left over for you, too."

Jamie shook his head. "You're amazing," he said with grudging admiration.

She eyed him seriously. "You, too. There's no way I could ever touch a snake. No way." She shook her head decisively while Jamie blushed and kicked a stone.

They left Ellen with Blackie and wandered out of the clearing. Scab shook himself free and ran back to the panther. Outside, word had spread. Others wanted to know: "What is it? What's going on?"

All afternoon the groups queued to take the oath and gasp in wide-eyed awe at Blackie's overwhelming size and her sleek blackness – blackness that shone out of her like a dark star.

And as the garden's quiet glades grew greyer in the evening light, so everyone grew more secure in the presence of the warm, soft coat. Children draped themselves on her as if she were a willing horse. They stroked her, and nosed into the deep, earthy, animal smell of fur, and only Scab resented it. He jealously bit an ankle that threatened too close; and drew blood from a finger that imagined – absurdly – that he, too, needed their affection.

The next day was the same; and the next.

"We know that they're not keeping the secret," said Lara, "or there wouldn't be so many people. Goodness knows what their parents are thinking. I don't know half of these kids; they must come from miles away.

"And that's another thing. We've got a mountain of catfood now. We can't keep feeding poor old Blackie on jellied fish. She should have something

108

to gnaw on. I've been down to the library and read about it. That's why they need bones. To keep their teeth good."

"And if we don't provide it who knows what she'll chew on. A customer, maybe . . . "

They sent Harry and Ellen to beg bones from the butcher's shop. The pair staggered back carrying a bag between them. Ellen moaned incessantly about having the heaviest side. Harry said she wasn't trying.

"I'm only small," she whined. "It's too big. We should've come back for half."

Harry raised his eyes to the sky. "What am I doing here anyway? You're so fond of telling everyone it's your pet."

"You're just jealous."

A shadow fell between them and a pair of hands reached down, purposefully taking hold of the bag straps. "Now, now kiddywinks; why don't you let me take it for you, while you tell me what the problem is?"

Sean again.

He towered between them; Mark and Chrissie flanked them on either side. There was nothing they could do; running was out of the question and they were too far away from home to yell. They relinquished their hold on the bag. Sean lifted it easily to his large bull-head, and peered in. "Bones eh? Opened the zoo again have we then? Taking people's money under false pretences again?" Harry and Ellen paled, but their mouths grew hard and they said nothing.

Sean looked down at each of them in turn and

growled menacingly. "I hear you've got somethin' special."

Harry and Ellen didn't dare look at each other. "Words out you've got a big cat; a lion or somethin' . . . "

Still nothing.

"Who are these bones for then, eh?"

Ellen's eyes blazed and she replied furiously, "They're for Feather and if you take them I'll get my brother on to you!"

Sean leered down at her and exchanged knowing glances with Mark and Chrissie. "Oh, we're not going to pinch 'em. We're goin' to deliver 'em for you, aren't we?"

The other two nodded. Chrissie shoved Ellen forward, Mark pushed Harry. The helpless pair stumbled on.

By the time they turned into the side alley the queue was already forming for the daily opening. When Harry thought he was close enough he grabbed Ellen and ran. They tore past the queue, shoved open the side gate and raced through, stumbling down the rough track leading into the undergrowth. Ellen's feet barely touched the ground as she was dragged after Harry.

"Sean's coming!" He yelled. "Jamie; Sean's coming!"

As they rounded a corner into the clearing first Jamie, then Feather, Emily and Lara, appeared ahead of them.

Harry slithered, gasping, to a halt; Ellen, too. "He's got Blackie's bones!" she cried indignantly.

Jamie sighed. "I suppose it had to happen. He strode to the side of the clearing, calling Feather to follow him. Once there, he ordered the dog to lie down out of sight behind a bush. Jamie returned to the centre of the clearing in time to hear Sean's bragging voice coming along the track.

As he came into sight he saw Jamie and his teeth showed in a humourless grin. "Well, here he is . . . the zookeeper. How are the animals?" He grinned pointedly round at the rest of the gang. Mark and Chrissie sniggered.

"I saw your little sister up the road and I've carried her bag of bones for her. Now . . ." Sean's face became grim, "you show me what they're for and I'll feed it, right?"

"Wrong," said Jamie.

Sean looked round. Seeing no sign of Feather, he became more menacing. "Listen, Jimmie-the-one. I've been hearing stories about you. You've told those kids out there you've got a lion or a panther or somethin'. Some of 'em even believe it. Well, that's not fair, see? And I'm going to find out what's goin' on."

"No you're not," said Jamie. "You're going to go away."

Sean glanced over Jamie's shoulder and saw a sign: "Mystery animal", pointing along a path. "Don't bother to show me the way," he scowled. "I'll find it myself."

Jamie stepped into his path.

"Listen, dozo," scowled Sean. "If you don't want to get hurt again you'd best step aside; or you're goin' to be eating these bones." He thrust the heavy bag under Jamie's nose.

Jamie said nothing, but whistled gently. Feather appeared immediately, the hair on his back stiff as wire, and a low growl growing in his throat as he crossed the clearing to join Jamie.

Sean's face dropped.

"You've got his bones," said Jamie, simply.

Feather stopped beside Jamie, head low, his growl deepening with every snatched breath. Sean stood, mouth shut, colour flaming in his cheeks, shuffling his feet. Jamie eyed him steadily, his face giving nothing away, while Sean's eyes flicked wildly from Jamie to Feather, and around the clearing.

With a scowl he thrust the bag forcefully into Jamie's chest, turned on his heel and left. Mark and Chrissie were already ahead of him.

Jamie reached down and fondly caressed Feather, who reverted to tongue-lolling adoration. Jamie reached into the bag, hauled out the biggest bone and dropped it in front of the dog, who dragged it off by one end, bottom waddling, tail wagging.

"Hey, they're for Blackie," wailed Ellen.

"Shut up, pain. Or would you like me to call Sean back?"

Ellen shut up.

"This is going to be a problem," frowned Lara. "He's obviously got wind of it. I can't see him letting it go just like that."

Jamie nodded agreement.

Emily nudged him playfully in the arm. "You *are*

good at handling snakes," she smiled. He grinned back at her.

"He's curious now," said Jamie. "He'll be back sometime. Me and Feather can't always be handy."

Emily shrugged. "Look, *he* thinks we're cheating on everyone. He doesn't believe there is a panther. So let's get on and open up, or that queue out there is going to break the gate down. Maybe something will occur to us before the day is over."

Nothing did occur to them. They fed and watered all the creatures, carefully shutting them in their enclosures for the night. Blackie and Scab curled together on their nest of rags while the mice skittered and scratched high on their shelf in the growing twilight. As the children locked the shed and headed home they had no idea how close the problem really was.

Nine

Night fell early in the shade of the overgrown gardens. Long before midnight the shed's interior was a thick pudding of darkness.

A near-full moon threaded its way in small, brief patches among the wilderness glades; but it could not penetrate the warm, pillow-deep darkness of the shed.

Out on the grass in their straw-filled, packing-crate kennel the foxcubs occasionally twitched a dreaming muscle. Inside only the mice were active, gnawing sticks, chewing paper, carrying straw.

Invisible in the blackness the black flank of the outstretched panther rose . . . and fell; rose . . . and fell. Scab's limp, dreamless body lay draped across her legs, pale, furred underbelly inelegantly exposed.

There was not silence, for the night is never silent of the cricking bugs, the secret whispering of leaves; but there was – peace.

A light swept the shed front; a round beam hit the dust-covered window, throwing a cobwebbed shadow on to the back wall. The beam snapped out.

The wind in the bushes yielded to a different sound, sharp and distant,

"Turn the torch back on!"

The light snapped on again, full into the snarling, squinting eyes of Sean. He felt for it blindly; snatched it from Mark's grasp.

"Not in my face, you idiot. How am I supposed to see anythin'?"

"Sorry, I didn't know it was pointing straight at you," hissed Mark.

Sean eased back a shrub and shone the torch. Once again it scanned the shed. "That's where it'll be; whatever it is. I betcha."

Behind them a twig snapped. Both boys jerked round, wide-eyed. Chrissie caught the torchlight full in the face, putting his hands up to protect his eyes.

In the shed the panther tensed. A black ear swivelled invisibly.

"Can't you be quiet?" seethed Sean. "We should've left you behind."

"It's ever so dark; are you sure they can't hear us," whispered Chrissie.

He heard Sean's scorn in the shadows. "Typical. You were so keen to come. Now you shut up and do what you're told. Course they can't hear us; not through all the bushes."

He swung the light back to the shed. Mark followed the track of the beam. "What if they have got something in there, Sean? You know; somethin' . . . dangerous."

Sean snorted. "No chance. It's a racket; an' I'm goin' to find out what."

"What if the dog's in there?"

"Huh! Row you're making it would have started barking by now."

Mark looked round nervously. "I dunno, Sean. It's a bit, kind of . . . eerie."

Sean rounded on them both, thrusting the torch beam into their faces. "Well you shoulda thought of that. We're goin' to find out what's in that shed; an' you're going to help. Come on."

He eased himself past the shrubs into the open. For Chrissie and Mark the choice was simple. Stay in the dark alone without the torch; or follow Sean into the dark with it. They followed Sean.

Inside the shed the black body raised itself, unceremoniously dumping the limp form of Scab. He woke with a soft mew as he hit the pile of clothes. He stretched himself and rubbed against Blackie's legs.

The torch played across the shed. Scab's ears went back and he bared his teeth in a silent scowl.

Outside, Sean was examining the window. He pressed the torch against the glass, but the thick dust on the inside prevented him seeing any detail inside. The ancient window had a single casement opening with a fanlight above. The whole of it was flaking paint and crumbling timber.

From his pocket he produced a screwdriver which he forced easily into the shrunken frame of the fanlight. Levering down, he heard the catch inside give way with a soft tearing sound.

He turned to Chrissie. "I'll give you a leg up. You should be able to reach in an' open the main window."

"Me," squeaked Chrissie. "But Sean —"

He waved the torch menacingly under Chrissie's nose. "Do it."

Chrissie used Sean's cupped hands as a stirrup to raise himself up. Peering through the fanlight slot he could hear only the stillness, see only the blackness.

Holding his breath he ducked his head through. "Urghh! It's got cobwebs." He pushed his arm through the opening and reached down, scrabbling for the catch. "It's stiff," he hissed.

He tugged, and tugged again. The catch grated, jerked a little, and pulled free. Chrissie half fell, half climbed back down from his perch. Sean abandoned him to tug at the window, frozen with age on its hinges. He forced the screwdriver into the gap and levered. The window opened stiffly a centimetre. He dropped the screwdriver and prised the frame wide open with his fingers.

"Wait here," he whispered. "I'm going in." He flicked the torch on. The beam hit the shelves over the workbench. A small pink nose ducked back out of sight into its nest.

Sean laughed hoarsely. "They've got mice," he scoffed. "Just flippin' mice. That can't be it."

He switched the beam off and swung himself over the window ledge, on to the shed floor. Had the torch been on as he swung down it would have reflected the burning yellow eyes of Blackie, padding curiously forward, and the glare of Scab treading alongside her, ears back, eyes narrowed, murder in his heart.

Sean paced across the floor. The torch snapped on again.

"There's nothing else here," he whispered back through the open window into the darkness where Mark and Chrissie stood, their hearts fluttering.

Sean swung back to the shelf with the mouse-cage on it, turning his back on the two cats as he did so. They watched him impassively, each tail flicking at its tip as he lifted the cage down to the workbench.

"Shouldn't keep things in cages," he grinned wickedly. "S'not fair." He wished he had hung on to the screwdriver. The torch beam swept the worktop, looking for an implement with which to force the cage bars. Behind him a feline nose, black and silky, quivered elegantly a few millimetres from the small of his back. Another, pink and scarred, sniffed distastefully at his sock.

The torch beam scanned the shelf above the workbench. Nothing there; maybe beneath it. Sean lowered the torch, stepping back to see.

The bloodcurdling scream of pain, as Scab's paw was trampled under Sean's heavy heel, was clearly heard that night by people in their beds two streets away. Jamie, Lara and Emily were immediately alert in their beds. Downstairs in Jamie's house Feather began to bark. Outside the shed Chrissie howled, clinging in terror to Mark. They hobbled clumsily back, tripped and fell together.

The ghostly caterwaul was cut off abruptly as the murderous tabby closed his fangs around Sean's ankle.

The boy's yell of terror thundered round the confines of the shed. The hairs on his neck stuck out like wire, his legs turned to string, and his arms thrashed the air in terror; but he kept a grip on the shining torch. Scab's teeth buried themselves in his leg again and Sean half-turned, half-tottered, expecting to see the spectre of the risen dead gripping at his ankles.

Instead the torchbeam blazed into the startled eyes and sculpted head of Blackie. Taken by surprise, inches from Sean, her face contorted in a fanged snarl.

Sean heard the harsh, fine hiss as the panther spat fear; he looked into the jagged cavern of its jaws. His eyes rolled back in his head and only the pain in his bitten ankle kept him from fainting. His howl of terror split the air. Chrissie and Mark picked themselves up and fled.

Jamie opened the back door and loosed the baying Feather into the garden's undergrowth.

Sean stumbled forward, tripped over Scab and crashed heavily to the wooden floor. Blackie screamed; Scab leapt on Sean's back and sank his fangs into the boy's ear.

By an extraordinary muscular effort, Sean hurled himself through the open window, the dark shape of Scab still clinging to his back.

Sean blundered, howling, across the clearing as Feather galloped into it from the far side. Sean fell through a bush, picked himself up and fled. Scab, still on the boy's back, was flaying his denim jacket to shreds with his hind claws. He growled into

Sean's bitten ear while Feather followed, snapping at his heels.

Jamie could still hear them through the blanket of shrubs when he arrived at the shed, his own torch in hand. He played the beam around the clearing, picking up the open window. Through it the yellow eyes peered back like fires.

"Blackie," he called cautiously, "Blackie? You all right then?" The eyes squinted lazily back, recognizing the voice. The deep chest began to build its rhythmic purr.

Jamie reached through and stroked her head. "There, girl. There, there." The purr deepened. He shone the torch into the shed and swept the beam through it; then around the clearing. He guessed it had been Sean.

"Well, at least you haven't killed him . . . have you?" He laughed nervously. "Feather won't hurt him; just frighten him a bit."

He remembered Scab and a frown creased his brow. "Where's Scab then," he said, partly to Blackie, partly to himself, "I hope he's okay, or Emily will go barmy. If they've hurt him I'll . . . "

A rustling in the bushes made him stop. He shone the torch in time to see Feather bound into view, tongue lolling, tail wagging. Behind him Scab stalked in; stiff legged, tail skyward, thick and bristly as a cactus. He growled as he approached. Bits of denim were threaded between his toes.

Jamie smiled. Scab leapt up at the window ledge, balanced there while he rubbed his face against Blackie's inquisitive nose, and dropped down inside.

Jamie heard a voice calling him. He swung the torch and caught the blinded figures of Lara and Emily at the clearing edge.

"We heard the noise and saw you run out," hissed Emily across the clearing. "What's going on?"

"Better ask them." He pointed to the animals. "Looks like they saw off a burglar."

"Do you think it was Sean?"

"Must have been. Who else would find their way in here?"

"Do you think he saw Blackie?" said Lara.

He shrugged. "Maybe. Hardly matters, though. He'll be after revenge either way."

They pondered the problem silently.

"Anyway," said Jamie. "He won't be back tonight. I think he got the worst of it. Give us a hand shutting things up. I'll check inside. Then we'd better get back before we're missed."

Lara woke them early the next morning with stones thrown at their windows. She beckoned them down urgently.

In the garden Ellen, who had slept through the excitement of the previous evening, examined Lara critically. "Why've you got breakfast down your T-shirt?"

"It's muesli, if you must know. I was in the middle of a spoonful when I heard the radio. I nearly choked. They announced on the news that Blackie's loose. Except they didn't call her Blackie.

121

She's called Princess and she *does* belong to the man in the paper; the one who didn't have a licence. Apparently the police arrived with a vet to take custody but it had escaped."

Emily snorted. "Humpf! The owner probably let her go on purpose. That's what I'd do if someone was coming to take her."

"Well; no-one's taking her away from here," said Ellen hotly. "She's my cat and I won't let them!"

The others all looked at one another, seriously concerned.

Harry said lamely: "At least no-one knows she's here."

"Don't be daft," scoffed Emily. "There isn't a kid in the neighbourhood that hasn't seen it!"

"But we made them take an oath . . . "

"Sure; and they went off and told all their friends. You know what kids are like: 'This is a secret so I'll tell you but don't tell anyone else.' And some of them are bound to have told their parents. They might not have listened before, but they'll listen now all right."

Jamie coughed. "And there's Sean."

The realization brought a gasp of horror from them.

"If he heard the radio, too, then he'll know the panther's real; and he'll tell. He'll do anything to get at us."

Harry blurted, "But that means they'll take her away and have her put down."

Lara, Jamie and Emily nodded.

Ellen stamped her feet. "They will not! not! not!"

her face was purple with indignation. "I'll take her and run away. They mustn't find her."

Lara laid her hand gently on Ellen's shoulder. "Hang on; there's a bit more: They're offering a reward. One thousand pounds. Dead or alive. They said on the radio. They talked to the police chief in charge. He said no-one should approach the panther. They should inform the police who – get this, this is the worst bit – who had a team of marksmen ready with rifles. He said public safety came first. They would catch it alive if possible; otherwise they'd have to shoot it. He said the courts had ordered it should be put down anyway."

Emily's eyes blazed furiously. "What do they know about anything! How can they be so stupid?" She kicked at the ground. "What are we going to do?"

"Give Blackie back?" suggested Harry.

He wilted as the others eyed him scornfully. "It's no good looking at me like that," he blushed. "We're not talking about Sean the brawn anymore. We're talking about the police; people with guns. It's getting a bit heavy."

Emily shouted, "We can't just give her up so they can destroy her. And what about Ellen? She's shown us all up. She was the only one who wasn't terrified of Blackie. And she's not giving up. I reckon we've got to do something to help."

"I've been thinking about that," said Lara. "If Sean was listening to the radio like I was, he could be on his way already. So, the first thing is to move Blackie – now; right . . . ?"

Sean arrived less than an hour later. They were outside the shed when they heard his voice. He was accompanied by two policemen who gingerly ducked the overhanging branches to avoid losing their peaked caps.

Lara stepped forward to meet them. "What's going on?" she asked, hoping her face carried the right air of bewilderment.

The policeman looked serious. One said, "Just making enquiries, miss." He looked around him. Emily was standing beside Sounds' hutch, with the rabbit in her arms, stroking its ears.

Feather stood beside Jamie, never taking his eyes from Sean, a low rumbling developing in his throat. Jamie ordered him to silence. Harry was standing by the closed door of the shed.

"Maybe you heard the news on the radio," said the second policeman. "There's a big cat on the loose. A panther. Probably won't come anywhere near here; but it could be dangerous."

Lara nodded. "That's why we're getting the animals inside," she said with a smile. "You couldn't give us a hand with the hutch could you; it's a bit heavy."

Harry's mouth dropped open at his sister's nerve, but the policeman smiled and walked forward. "Pleasure."

The other policeman blushed faintly and said, "This young man says he was attacked here yesterday, in that shed; by a . . . er . . . by a panther."

Sean smirked, unseen by the policemen. The others looked at each other and laughed. Sean's round face went beetroot with fury.

"If it's so funny why don't you open the shed —" he began, but the policeman waved him sharply to silence.

He'd met plenty of lads like Sean; you could see the bully lurking. Usually their complaints were shallow whining because things hadn't turned out their way. Best to let it go; let the kids sort it out among themselves.

But there had been something about the urgency in Sean's voice, his description of the attack, that had been convincing.

On the other hand, that laugh just then. It was too . . . immediate; too . . . staged.

"Well, as it's so funny," he said. "You won't mind us looking in the shed will you?"

Lara blushed. "No, of course not." She wrenched open the door. The policeman peered in the entrance. The shed was full of creatures. The foxcubs somersaulted across the floor in front of their kennel. Cuddles snuffled in the corner of a makeshift pen. On the workbench the mynah bird's cage stood with both the mynah and the crow peering out, listening with cocked heads. There was the guinea pig in its hutch and the two mice in their cage. The grass snake was a camouflaged green rope still as a stick in its vivarium; but there was no panther. Only Scab, sitting facing the shed door, twitching his kinked tail.

Lara explained each of the creatures in turn. Lastly she said, "He's Scab. He's a stray, really; but he seems to have adopted us. Well, Emily.

I – er – I shouldn't go too close. He's not very friendly."

"You shouldn't really keep wildlife penned up, you know," said the policeman, pushing his cap back on his head.

"Oh, but we don't," Emily interrupted. "Really. The fox cubs had lost their parents so we're just rearing them. When they're big enough we'll let them go. And the crow was shot in the wing by . . . " She stopped, thinking better of it. "Shot in the wing, and we're only nursing him. He'll fly off as soon as he's fit. But if he wasn't in that cage he really would be a goner."

Sean had listened to all he could take. "It *was* here," he shouted. "They must've moved it. That cat was here, too."

"Quiet," ordered the policeman.

He looked at the others. "Well?"

They shook their heads.

"You can't listen to all this," Sean interrupted. "They're havin' you on. It was definitely here. I had the torch right on its face. If I hadn't jumped through the window —"

"What were you doing with a torch?" asked the policeman.

Sean paused. This was going the wrong way. "It was . . . er . . . a bit dark."

"It's always locked after dark," said Jamie quietly.

The other policeman rounded on Sean. "So what were you doing inside then; break in, did you?"

Sean ignored him. He nodded his head towards

Scab. "An' look what that cat's done to my ear. It needs putting down –"

"I thought you said it was a panther that attacked you?".

"And the cat; both of them." Sean looked from one policeman to the other, his face flushed. "They've hidden it somewhere. Look around. It's got to be here." He poked his head inside the shed door, and Scab spat fiercely.

Sean scowled at Emily. "If that thing touches me," he hissed, "I'll shoot it."

"Like you did the crow?" Emily baited him.

"Yeah; only I'll do more than wing it."

A hand gripped his shoulder firmly. "Out of it, you," said the policeman. "It's time we had a bit of a chat."

He pulled Sean firmly back out of the shed and signalled to the other policeman that they were leaving.

He turned to the four children. "Seems like we got the wrong story," he smiled grimly.

They nodded, wide-eyed with innocence.

The policeman hesitated, then turned back and said, "Just one thing. If you did come across this panther you wouldn't do anything foolish, would you? It could be very dangerous; no matter what anyone says. And you'd be breaking the law. It's illegal to keep a wild animal without a licence."

They shook their heads.

The policemen left. Sean was between them, protesting injustice all the way.

Once they were alone Emily hugged Lara. "You

were brilliant! They'll never believe anything he says ever again."

"You were all great!"

"Never mind that," said Jamie. "Let's go and tell Ellen it's all right to come out now."

Ten

They raced to Jamie's house and barged in through the back door. Jamie came to a sudden stop and the others cannoned into him like wagons behind a braking train.

"Hello, dear," said his mother as she closed a kitchen drawer. "You all right? You look a bit pale."

All the colour had drained from Jamie's face. "What are you doing here? I thought you'd gone shopping."

"Missed the bus."

She called beyond Jamie's tall figure to the others. "Hello, you lot. You can come in, you know. I won't bite." They filed in with Jamie. "My, you do look a serious lot."

She peered past Harry, the last in the queue. "Where's Ellen?" Her voice took on a new urgency. "She's all right, isn't she?"

Jamie groaned. "Yes Mum, of course. She's – er – upstairs. I think. She wanted to . . . umm . . . go to the loo. We'll go and see she's all right." He ducked past her into the hall and leapt the stairs three at a time. The others were at his heels.

"And don't think you can be running through the kitchen all day. I've got baking to do," his mother called as she lined up ingredients along a worktop.

The group reached the top of the stairs, crossed the landing and thrust open a door, piling through into Ellen's bedroom.

It was a big, light, airy room, with a bed in one corner covered with a picturebook sunshine cover. The furnishings had been placed to give lots of central space for Ellen to play.

She was in the middle of this space, a beam of delight on her face, her legs straddling Blackie's sleek back.

"Look at me. It's easy. I had to climb on the bed, but she kept ever so still," she said gleefully.

The door had been pushed shut. Jamie leaned against a wall, ignoring his sister. "We're never going to get away with this," he groaned.

Ellen was oblivious. "Giddyup," she called, jogging her body. Blackie began to pad slowly forward.

"Couldn't we sneak out the front door?" offered Emily.

"And into the street. Oh great! That would really be secret, wouldn't it?"

"Sorry, I'm sure. I'm only trying to help. I don't hear anything better from you," grumbled Emily.

"Even nothing's better than that," snapped Jamie. "This is serious. If my mum walks in on this . . . the shock could be terminal!"

"Stop arguing," interrupted Lara. "There must

be some way." She crossed to the window and looked down on the garden below. Too high.

Ellen continued urging Blackie round the room. "I'm the king of the castle . . . "

Lara eyed her thoughtfully. An idea was forming. "We'll need a sheet, a big one; and we'll have to cut a couple of holes in it."

In the kitchen Jamie's mother could hear whispering on the landing. She sensed the stubbornness in Jamie's voice although she couldn't make out the words. Low, tense tones drifted down the stairs. She heard Emily cajoling and Lara reasoning; Harry giggled.

The only clear voice was Ellen's: "I'm the king of the castle . . . "

"What are you lot plotting?" her mother called gaily. The whispering stopped. A few seconds later she heard them progressing clumsily down the stairs. More whispering. She left the bowl of half-beaten eggs and, wooden spoon in hand, went into the hall.

A white apparition was heading down the stairs, with Lara below it, easing it along. Ellen straddled its back, trying to wriggle free of Emily's caring arms as she held her in place.

"I'm all right, I can do it on my own," she whined.

Harry came behind. His job was to keep the sheet which covered Blackie from slipping off, or tripping the panther. Jamie was nowhere to be seen.

His mother smiled. "I hope you're taking care of my sheet. I don't want it ripped."

Lara moved adroitly to shield Blackie's head, where the yellow moons of her eyes peered out through two rough-cut holes in the fabric.

She tugged at the head. "Of course," she laughed nervously. "Come on, Bla – er Jamie, that is."

They reached the bottom of the stairs and skirted round Ellen's mother. She said, "That's a big horse. What do you call it?"

"It's not a horse, it's a panther and it's a she and her name's Blackie," said Ellen grandly, from her seat.

"Well, you'd better tell it to gallop through the kitchen. I've got work to do." As the group moved slowly past she raised the wooden spoon and gave the sheet-covered rump a robust clout.

Blackie spun round, spitting in blind alarm.

132

Emily was knocked to the floor. Ellen slid sideways off the panther's back, dragging the sheet with her. Lara screamed as Blackie's sleek flank slid into view. Harry did the only thing that came to mind; he threw the sheet over Ellen's mother. She disappeared, shrieking, beneath it.

Ellen landed heavily on Emily, banged her head on the kitchen wall and howled. Blackie arched her back and scowled in wide-mouthed fear as she backed down the kitchen towards the garden door.

"I'm ever so sorry," Harry was saying to Ellen's mother. She struggled to get out of the sheet; he struggled to keep her under it. "Hang on, it's tangled," he lied. He signalled urgently to Lara to get Blackie out.

She opened the door with one hand, desperately shoving Blackie through with the other. The big cat wouldn't budge.

"If you'd just let me get up," gasped Ellen's mother. Harry kept one hand on her head and jabbed a finger towards Ellen with the other. "She won't go without Ellen," he whispered urgently.

Lara nodded understanding; grabbed the howling Ellen off the floor, where she was still sitting on Emily's head, and shot out of the door with her. Blackie spun round and followed them swiftly across the concrete into the undergrowth at the garden's edge.

"Now just a MINUTE!" roared Ellen's mother from under the sheet. The tone brooked no argument or discussion. Everything went quiet. Harry stepped back. The shrouded figure struggled to a crouch and then smartly to attention. A hand beneath grabbed at the sheet and tugged it free. It floated to the ground, conveniently covering the two eye holes, and left the woman flushed and tousled, looking breathlessly around her.

She narrowed her eyes in the silence and looked first to Harry, and then to Emily, still stretched out on the floor.

"What's going on?" she said, suspiciously.

"Er . . . nothing," said Harry. "I think you gave Bla – . . . er . . . Jamie a fright. I better go and find them." He bolted past her to the door.

"Me too," said Emily. She clambered up and fled after him.

Ellen's mother shook her head. Putting the wooden spoon down, she picked up the sheet and folded it. She headed for the stairs. "Kids," she muttered.

At the top of the stairs she met Jamie, heading down. She stopped, mouth open.

"Hi!" said Jamie, gaily. He continued down the stairs.

"I thought you were outside?"

"Been to the loo," he called back. "See you."

She watched him go, bewildered.

She opened a cupboard door and smoothed the folded sheet in her hands before placing it inside, turning it as she did so. Her fingers caught in the two ragged holes.

Jamie was already through the back door when the boom of her voice caught him in its angry shock wave.

"JAMES!"

He didn't stop.

They were all safely in the shed when he caught up with them. Blackie had calmed down and was rubbing her long head against Ellen, nearly knocking her over. "She's found the sheet," he muttered.

There was a pause. They all waited; knowing what was to be said, and by whom, for it would take the sensible one among them to put it into words.

"We can't go on like this much longer," said Lara. "It's getting too close."

There was silence, broken by Ellen who threw an arm over Blackie and snorted. "You can all do what you like; but she's mine and I'm not giving her up. Not ever."

Emily looked at her gently. "Don't you see? We've had two lucky escapes today; lots of people know she's here. It won't be long before the police realize Sean was right. They'll be back."

Ellen rubbed her cheek against Blackie's head, saying nothing.

Harry pressed his nose against the window and said: "If I was a millionaire I'd turn this whole place into a wildlife park and we could have every kind of animal we wanted. It'd be like Noah's Ark." He laughed and looked round at them. "We could call it Noah's Park!"

The others laughed a little, too, but their hearts weren't in it. They sat forlornly, searching for a way forward. The only sound was Blackie's deep, throaty rumble of contentment.

Emily's head cocked, as if she was listening to a far-off sound. In a way she was, but it was coming from inside her head. The sound of an idea forming.

"Maybe that's the answer," she said. "A wildlife park. Like Longleat. If we could get Blackie into somewhere like that, surely they'd leave her in peace."

Jamie shook his head, scornfully, "You've just glossed over the hard bit. How do we get her there? On the train, maybe?"

"Mum and Dad are always saying they'll take me to Longleat. If we could sneak Blackie into the car . . . it's a station wagon; it's big enough."

The others were taking notice. All except Ellen, who was turned away with her nose buried in the comforting warmth of Blackie's coat.

"We could cover her with a blanket or something," said Lara. "It might work."

Harry shook his head. "I don't see how Emily can manage it on her own. And Blackie isn't going to go anywhere far without Ellen."

"We'll all have to go." Emily was up on her knees now, excitement mounting. "We can even pay if we have to. We've got money from the zoo. They'll do it. They owe me an outing. It would have to be a weekend though, because of Dad's work."

"It would have to be *this* weekend," added Jamie. "The police won't shrug their shoulders and give up; not until they find what they're looking for. You don't leave a panther on the loose and forget about it."

"It's a bit short notice. You know what it's like.

It takes two days going on about it before they make up their mind."

Harry groaned. "You, too. I thought only ours were like that."

"And it would have to be Sunday. The tiles all fell off the bathroom last week. Dad's repairing them on Saturday . . . "

Her voice trailed away. She was looking across the shed to Ellen, whose head was turned into the panther's black flank. Her shoulders heaved and shook.

Lara moved over to her and tried to coax her gently round. Ellen tugged herself free and continued weeping with her head buried against Blackie.

"Ellen, please don't," pleaded Lara. "Please . . . "

The small girl rounded on them, each eye wearing a red rim of tears. Blackie's flank was streaked with wet. "It's cos I found her and you're jealous. You want to get rid of her. Why don't you help me hide her 'stead of making plans to send her away?"

"Oh Ellen, we'd love to keep her. We're not jealous, really we're not. But we can't hide her forever."

Emily added, "Apart from anything else we can't afford to feed her unless people pay to see her; so if we hide her she'll starve."

"She can have all my share. And my pocket money. I don't mind," Ellen sniffed. She wiped her nose along her arm and rubbed her arm down her dress.

Lara turned to Emily. "Go now. Try to fix up the outing. Keep on until they give in. We won't get another week before they come looking again. It's got to be now, and it's got to be all of us. I reckon it'll take that many to keep Blackie hidden on the way."

Emily looked down forlornly at Ellen, who still sobbed into Blackie's warm flank. "Don't worry," said Jamie, "We'll take care of her. Good luck."

A smile passed between them before Emily turned and ran for home.

Eleven

Emily had two days to persuade her parents. She trailed her mother round the house all afternoon. "But why not, Mum? You said you would; and we haven't done anything. Not a thing all summer holidays."

"We said we would when we were straight," her mother replied yet again, her patience rapidly diminishing.

"But that'll be years," groaned Emily. "I mean, just look around you."

Her mother did. "Yes, well; it takes a while; but you'll see. It'll come together in a rush one day; and then we can spend the weekends doing whatever you want."

"That's what you said in the last house," said Emily firmly. "And as soon as it was half-way finished you sold it and bought this place. I bet the same thing happens again. I bet!"

Her mother turned to look at her. "I know it's hard on you, darling. But we're so short of money. If we weren't we'd buy somewhere that was already done up."

"It won't cost a thing. I can pay for myself; you, too, if you like."

Her mother sighed, "We don't want you to pay; it's not really the money."

"You just said it was."

"No, no . . . it's just . . . Look, we'll see; all right? "I'm not promising," she added hastily as Emily's face lit up. "It's up to Dad."

It was the following day – Saturday – before Emily had a chance to work on her father. She dogged his footsteps all morning and all afternoon as he continued the bathroom repairs. She carried his tape measure, handed him tiles and tile adhesive, keeping up a constant barrage, "Please, Dad; please? I'll pay for myself, please?"

He finally lost his temper as a section of tiling slowly parted company with the wall and fell with a crash into the bath. He moved to save them and trod in the pot of adhesive. He threw down the gluey plastic blade he was using to layer the adhesive on to the tiles, and it stuck to his shoe.

Emily grabbed a cloth and lifted his leg. "Never mind, I'll clean it off for you."

He unbalanced and slid down the wall.

"That's it!" he barked. "All day you've nagged and nagged and I have had it up to here." He indicated a point above his head; but from where he sat it didn't reach any higher than Emily. He struggled up. Emily backed against a wall as he hobbled angrily towards her, the adhesive pot still stuck to his shoe.

"If you will get out now, immediately," he fumed, "without another word, I give you my solemn promise I will take you anywhere in the world you wish to go. In fact the further the better. On the other hand, if you stay I'm going to brick you into this bathroom forever!"

Emily couldn't believe what she was hearing. She tried to hide her grin. Don't overdo it, she told herself. Get out while you're ahead. "Wow, thanks Dad. I'll go and tell the others."

He stopped in the middle of reaching for the adhesive pot. "Woah, woah, woah–woah–woah."

Emily woahed.

"What others?" he growled suspiciously.

"Jamie and Lara and Harry and Ellen, of course. You didn't think I could go without them." He opened his mouth but she carried on. "We've done everything together this holiday. It's all right. They can pay for themselves; and we'll organize the picnic."

"Damn it, Emily; you've tricked me into this." He gave way to frustration and banged the bath with his fist. The sound gonged round the bathroom.

"Careful, Dad. You'll have the other tiles off."

The adhesive pot flew through the open door and hit the opposite wall of the landing, spattering its remaining contents over the wallpaper. Emily wasn't there any more.

She was downstairs, out through the bushes and into the garden to tell the others.

Relief flooded their faces. Only Ellen took the news badly. Emily found her in the shed lying full length along Blackie's back. The little girl listened quietly, said nothing.

"I'm sorry, Ellen. Really I am. But you know they'd never let us keep her here, don't you?"

Ellen nodded her head, letting a tear roll free. "I've never had my own pet before," she whispered.

Emily studied her. "Is that why you're upset."

Ellen shrugged. "I don't know. P'raps a bit. But I don't want anyone to hurt Blackie." Some of her old fierceness returned and she said through gritted teeth, "I won't let them; stupid people!"

Emily took her hand. "Look Ellen. When this is all over we'll get you another pet. Something special. I don't know what; but we can try. Will that help?"

Ellen smiled. "Nothing will ever be as good as Blackie. She gives me rides. Even a pony wouldn't be as good as Blackie."

Emily squeezed her hand and left the small girl to her sadness in the gathering gloom. There were things to be prepared for the trip to Longleat. They made sandwiches and they crept into the garage and threw coats and blankets into the back of the station wagon. "We're going to need as much as possible to cover Blackie," said Lara.

It was dark by the time they said goodnight to each other.

Next morning Emily woke her parents with tea and toast in bed. She wasn't risking them changing their minds. It had happened before.

"Morning," she sang briskly.

Her father groaned and covered his head with a pillow. Her mother woke, bewildered. "What the . . . " She snatched up the alarm clock. "It's seven o'clock on a Sunday morning, for God's sake."

"I know, but you can get up at your leisure, enjoy the tea, and the toast. We don't have to leave until nine."

"Why so early!"

"It's a long way. It'll take us an hour and a half the way Dad drives."

Emily crossed to the curtains and flung them back as her mother said: "I do wish you'd stop being so rude about your father . . . "

Emily had frozen at the window. One hand was high on the curtain and the light streamed in across her face as she stared down into the street.

"Did you hear me?" her mother repeated.

"Pardon . . . ?"

"Never mind, thanks for the tea."

Emily was oblivious to the words. Her eyes were fixed on a figure across the road leaning against the brick pillar of a garden wall. Sean.

He hadn't noticed her. His head turned as he glanced up and down the road. His hands were in his pockets as he slouched. She watched him closely, knowing his presence there so early could only mean trouble.

"Emily, what are you staring at?" called her mother.

Emily suddenly woke up to the world around her. The others; she had to tell the others.

"Oh . . . er . . . nothing. Just wondered if the weather was going to be any good." She continued to draw back the curtains and sunlight flooded in, staining the yukky-pink room to yellow.

She glanced to where her mother was sitting

upright, nibbling a piece of toast. Her father was still an indeterminate shape under the covers. "Don't let him be late, Mum. Please," she pleaded.

Her mother nodded as she nibbled and urged Emily gently from the room with a gesture of her free hand.

Had Emily waited a few more moments she would have seen a canvas-topped Landrover cruise to a halt beside Sean. She would have seen Sean talking to the driver – a man wearing green and khaki camouflage clothes – pointing out to him Emily's own house and those of Jamie and Ellen, Harry and Lara.

She would have seen him point further along the road, to where the side lane led to the back of the houses, and the jungle of their back gardens.

The driver was a lean man, impassive, with a tough, leathery, tanned face. He beckoned Sean into the vehicle. Sean ran around to the passenger side, climbed in, and the Landrover turned in the street and headed back towards the side lane Sean had pointed out.

Emily was already half-way down the stairs to alert the others. She met them at the back door. They were dressed and ready to go. She told them about Sean's presence.

Ellen was aghast. "He might be in the garden now!"

"I don't think so." Emily shook her head. "It was almost as if he was waiting for something."

"Whatever it is, we don't want to be here when it turns up." said Jamie. "I vote we get Blackie in the station wagon now, just in case."

"But we're not leaving for an hour and a half," said Lara. "She'll get bored in there all that time. She'll be ready to get out again by then. That'll look good half-way down the motorway: a panther licking Emily's Dad's neck."

"Look," said Jamie, irritably. "There's a reward out now. This isn't like the foxcubs, where you get a finger wagging for being somewhere you shouldn't. There's no knowing what crazy things people will do for money. We've got to get going. Now."

"I agree with Jamie," said Emily. She caught the look in Jamie's face. "Don't act so surprised. You're the stubborn one, not me."

The landrover engine subsided to silence as the driver switched off the ignition. He looked across at Sean. Ever since the operations centre telephone number had been published the team of police and professional marksmen had been kept busy with a string of false alarms. You could generally tell, thought the driver, when someone really was certain about a thing, and when they were just blustering. He wasn't keen on this boy's face. Couldn't say why, really. Just the sullen look, maybe. But he seemed to carry a genuine conviction that he'd seen the panther.

"What did you say your name was, son?"

"Sean."

"Okay, Sean. I'm Dan. You tell me exactly where this shed is, right?"

"I'll take you . . ."

"No. Sorry; but these are the rules: panthers are

145

deadly. They're experts at ambush. They've been known to double back on their prey and attack from above, from trees. They can leap enormous distances; the height of a house. I don't know what stories you've heard about this one being friendly; but believe me, it can't be true."

"You do *exactly* as I say. See this? It's a Lee Enfield .303 bolt action hunting rifle. It fires these." He fished into the box and pulled out a bullet. It was as big as Sean's middle finger. "I shan't use it unless I have to. It's a powerful, dangerous weapon."

He lifted another weapon. "I'll try and knock it out with this. It's a tranquilizer gun. But I can't take any chances. Especially if you say there are kids around. I don't want to have you to worry about, too."

He hesitated. "Besides; we don't want to start a panic, especially if you're mistaken —"

"It's there all right," scowled Sean, remembering the hot breath in his face, and his terror-stricken flight through the hut window. On reflection, he was happy to wait in the Landrover.

Both Scab and Blackie were nuzzling at the shed door when the gang opened it.

Ellen flung her arms round the big cat's neck and the insistent note of its purring began. Scab was less demonstrative, but he climbed up the legs of Emily's jeans until she winced with pain and hauled him off with her hands. Once gathered in her arms he, too, began to purr.

146

"I guess we better feed them first," she said.

"No. Take the tins to the car," insisted Jamie. "We can feed them in the garage. I don't want to hang around here. It's too vulnerable."

"Aren't you overdoing it a bit?" Emily caught the impatience in Jamie's face. "All right, all right." She put down Scab, who sat preening himself disdainfully, and turned to Ellen who had climbed on to Blackie's back. "Come on; bring your pussy-cat; time to go. Harry, will you grab some tins?"

Lara loaded them in his arms until they reached his chin. She picked up the tin-opener and stuffed it into his back pocket as he turned to go. "Don't forget this, idiot."

"Smart thinking," he mumbled, with his chin resting on top of the precarious stack.

She turned to Jamie. "We'd better feed all the other animals. We can't leave them all day without anything."

Jamie nodded. "You get started. I'll see Blackie safely into the car."

He followed Emily and Harry out. They hadn't gone very far. Emily was shoving at Blackie with Ellen on the big cat's back, but the animal refused to move. She was looking back at the shed.

"I don't get it. She won't budge," panted Emily.

Jamie groaned. "Now's a great time. We've got to move her. Lara!" he called.

Lara moved into the doorway. Scab idled forward beside her, mildly curious. As soon as Blackie saw the tabby, her ears pricked and her body tensed, eagerly alert. Emily noticed the sudden interest.

"Hang on," she said. "I think it's Scab. It's Scab she wants! Watch this." Emily ran over to Scab, picked him up and moved out of sight into the shed. Immediately Blackie began to backtrack past Jamie, towards the shed.

"I think you're right," said Jamie. "Okay, quick; get in front with Scab. Maybe Blackie will follow."

Emily did so. Sure enough, Blackie nosed into her arms for Scab as he was carried past. The panther eagerly padded after with Ellen bouncing on her back like a sack. Emily and Scab led the way out of the clearing to the house. James followed and Harry stumbled after him, peering over the stack of tins as he went.

The marksman cautiously parted the branches on the far side of the clearing. He saw the tall, willowy form of a boy run into the undergrowth. Another, smaller boy, followed carrying what looked like tins. The clearing appeared empty, apart from the shed.

He heard a noise and stiffened. Lara carried out a sack of oats from which to feed Sounds. She made off with it towards the hutch.

He retreated into the bushes and set off silently to reconnoitre the overgrown gardens.

Emily checked her parents were both upstairs, preparing for the outing, before the hidden group dashed across the small concreted yard, and through the garage door. By the pale light of a single bulb they fed tin after tin of jellied sardines to Scab and Blackie, secreting the remaining tins into the back of the car. Emily hid the empty tins behind some paint pots on a shelf.

It was almost time to leave when Lara finally joined them. They coaxed Blackie into the flat platform at the rear of the station wagon by lifting Ellen and Scab in first. Blackie followed, sniffing suspiciously at every step, ears back, head low. Once she was in beside Ellen they persuaded the big cat to lie down. They threw coats over her body and Ellen snuggled into her side. Scab strutted importantly over their covered shapes, kneading the coats with his claws.

Jamie opened a side door for Feather. The dog slunk in and curled up in the footwell.

"Do you think that's wise?" asked Lara. "If Emily's parents see him they may start looking around for more stowaways."

"He comes." Jamie's tone brooked no argument. "We couldn't have managed without him once or twice. He's not getting left out now."

The others shrugged and left the matter. In any case, time had run out. They could hear Emily's parents. The up-and-over door scraped open, flooding the garage with light. Blackie raised her head to see what the new sounds were. Emily leapt in the back alongside Ellen, threw a coat over the sleek black head and grabbed Scab as he was about to climb on the back of the rear seat. He spat at her, but didn't resist.

"Right!" her father's voice echoed round the garage. "Are we ready? Who's sitting where?" Jamie flew into a rear seat, his legs covering Feather.

149

Emily's father peered in after him. "You're a bit tall to sit there, Jamie. Why don't you stretch out right in the back?"

"Er, I'm fine, thanks."

Lara slammed the tailgate shut and she and Harry piled in beside Jamie on the far side.

"We're all ready," called Emily, "Let's go."

"Not so fast," said her father. "Is the food packed?"

"It's all in the back here. Come *on*, Dad."

He sniffed the air. "Are you taking fish sandwiches?"

"No, why?"

"Strong smell of fish in here . . . "

The sardines! Lara exchanged a horrified glance with Emily, but her father dismissed it, shook his head absently, and got in the driver's seat. The car roared into life and the noise jerked Blackie upright. She banged her head on the roof and scowled silently through wide jaws before Emily could drag her down.

In his rear-view mirror her father saw the shape rise up, and mistook it for Ellen. "Sorry," he called back. "I should have warned you I was starting up."

He drove out. Emily's mother closed the garage door, climbed into the passenger seat beside her husband and they set off. They drove slowly away, gathering speed past the side lane where the Landrover was still parked. They didn't see it. Their heads were turned to the rear of the car, breathlessly concerned that Blackie should stay down out of sight.

150

They didn't see Sean, either; but he saw them.

The marksman squatted on his haunches deep in the garden's shadowy depths, and examined an area of rich, earth-smelling leaf mould. At one edge was a clear paw print, much bigger than a dog's – and cat–shaped. The boy Sean had been telling the truth. The panther had been there, and the spoor was still clean; it must have been recently made.

He had been all over the garden, found all the creatures the children were caring for, found the painted signs advertising the wildlife park and the mystery animal; found, too, the growing pile of empty catfood tins.

He scratched his cheek reflectively. Maybe this big cat *was* tame . . .

He straightened up. But then again, maybe not. The safest course, he reminded himself, was in assuming it was lethal, especially if there were children around. He took a firmer grip on the rifle.

Back at the Landrover Sean waited eagerly for his return.

"Well, you were right," said Dan. "It's been there for sure. But it's not there now. I've been all over."

Sean banged the dashboard in front of him with frustration. "Damn! It must have been in the car."

The marksman eyed him quizzically.

"They just drove away," explained Sean. "The whole lot, with a couple of the parents."

"And a panther, sitting up on the back seat? We're not talking about the family dog, you know."

Sean blushed. "They've probably hidden it. I know 'em."

"Any idea where they went?"

"No, but it couldn't have been more than fifteen, twenty minutes ago."

Dan groaned, reaching for the radio. "Great! They'll be miles away. I guess I'd better put out an alert."

"Not yet." Sean opened the Landrover door and jumped down. "Hang on. I've got an idea." He ran round to the front of the houses, up to the first front door and hammered on it. Silence. He hammered again. He heard steps and the door flung open.

Lara and Harry's mother looked down at him, irritation on her face. She was wearing a dressing gown.

"I'm a friend of your kids," he lied. "Are they in?"

"They've gone to Longleat for the day with the children next door."

Sean was already tearing back down the garden path to the front gate. "And another time don't call so early on a Sunday morning," he heard Lara's mother call after him.

He flung himself into the Landrover. It coughed into life and set out on the road to Longleat.

Twelve

In the station wagon an urgent, whispered conversation was in progress about the next step, once they were inside the wildlife park.

In the front seats Emily's parents were bickering.

"Maybe you're just getting a cold," Emily's father said to his wife.

"I know a cold from an allergy," she replied haughtily, wiping her nose on a tissue. "This is too sudden. It only ever happens around cat hairs. You must have left the car window open. A stray's been in here."

"I *know* what cat hairs do to you, my love," he said testily. "That's why I *never* leave the windows open."

Her eyes streamed. She blew her nose violently on the tissue.

"Anyway," her husband continued. "We'll be there in half an hour; and you can get out."

In the back, Scab was bored. He wanted to take a look around the outside world. Emily tried to haul him down, but he yowled indignantly.

"Pardon, dear?" her mother called over her shoulder. Emily pretended she was playing a game with Ellen.

She yowled a few times to prove it. They let Scab peer through the rear window, to the delight of the passengers in the car behind. Blackie grew bored, too. She raised herself up on her forelegs and peered round. A coat was draped over her head and from the car behind she looked like another passenger who had sat up after taking a rest. Emily groaned. The yellow eyes watched the countryside speeding by. They picked up their own reflection in the driver's rear-view mirror. Blackie tried to climb over the seats to get a closer look. Jamie, Harry and Lara sat bolt upright, pressing together to shield the panther from the driver's view in the mirror.

Emily's father glanced up. "Can you children sit a bit lower?" he called. "You're blocking my view." His eyes flicked back to the road ahead as Blackie, curious at the sound of the new voice, nosed between the row of shielding heads and peered at Emily's parents.

With Ellen's help Emily dragged the big cat down. "Quick," she hissed. "Give me the tin opener."

Harry passed it. Rapidly she opened a tin of catfood. Blackie stood up to get her nose into it. Emily croaked quietly, hand clapped to her forehead, eyes closed, certain it was all over. Ellen slid a blanket over the muscled back. Jamie grabbed it from the far side and pulled it down.

"What *is* going on?" called Emily's father, frowning into the mirror at the bulk that was hidden by the blanket. The all-pervading smell of fish took his mind off it. "There's that smell again. I hope none of you lot have got anything unpleasant on your shoes."

154

Harry came to the rescue. "I remember now. My mum gave me sardine sandwiches. The wrapping must have come open."

"The sooner you eat them the better," snorted Emily's father. "Now Emily, stop fooling around and sit down so I can see out the back. Really! Your friends are better behaved than you."

"Sorry." She was on the far side, prising Blackie's nose out of the catfood tin while trying to force her on to her belly. Finally, with Ellen's help, she did it.

She shook the tin until its contents slid out on to the carpeted floor of the car's rear platform. The smell got worse.

"The sooner we get there the better," her father muttered, winding a window open. Her mother sneezed quietly, a soggy tissue pressed to her nose.

The Landrover had driven flat out. Flat out in a heavy Landrover isn't very fast, but it was faster than Emily's father drove.

Dan and Sean reached the far end of the motorway without spotting the station wagon. Sean's brief view as it had motored past had not given him time to identify it properly. All they knew was that it was a station wagon and it was red.

Once off the motorway they were unable to overtake. The Landrover had no speed to accelerate past vehicles, and the road was too narrow in most places anyway.

The driver glanced at the milometer. "Well, if we don't see them soon we've had it. It can't be more than ten minutes to Longleat."

He reached for the radio. "I'd better alert the other crews while we've got a chance."

"Let's give it a bit longer," urged Sean. "They can't be far ahead."

"We don't even know for sure they came this way. There are other wildlife parks. It could be a mistake—"

Sean cut him short, exploding with triumph. "There they are!"

A lorry had turned off, three cars ahead of them. When it cleared the main road the red station wagon was in full view; the fourth vehicle.

Another car followed the lorry. There were only two cars between them and the station wagon. Dan nodded, a flicker of a smile crossed his face. "We still don't know if the panther's on board; but we'll stay here until we get a chance to find out."

As he spoke one of the cars ahead slowed and pulled off the road into a layby. At the same time a rare gap appeared in the traffic approaching from the opposite direction. Dan rammed the Landrover hard into low gear and stamped on the throttle, swerving out to overtake the car in front. Sean gripped the dashboard hard, nervously studying the traffic that rushed up on them as the Landrover swerved back to its own side, cutting in on the car they had overtaken. Its driver sounded his horn.

The noise blared out, penetrating to Blackie where she lay covered with a blanket. She lifted her head to track down the sound. The blanket slid from her elegant head as she peered out through the rear window, full into the triumphant face of Sean and the stunned face of the marksman.

The noise of the car horn had prodded Ellen's attention, too. She turned to see the Landrover swerve back to the correct side of the road, and looked away. She blinked. The faces in the car came to life on her closed eyelids: a face she didn't know – and a face she did. She looked again. Sean grinned wickedly at her. The driver was staring open-mouthed at Blackie. She saw him pick up a radio handset. As he spoke into it, she screamed.

The noise made Emily's father jump. "For God's sake! How am I supposed to drive with you all acting like lunatics!"

The others turned. Ellen was pointing through the rear window. As Longleat had drawn closer, and they tried desperately to hide Blackie from Emily's parents, they had forgotten there were other dangers. Driving away from home they had silently imagined they were leaving the threat of Sean behind. Their spirits choked to silence as they watched him smirking from the vehicle behind.

"Damn!" breathed Jamie. He had turned in time to see the radio replaced on the dashboard. "It'll be all over southern England by now."

"He looks like one of those hunter people," wailed Ellen. "He's going to shoot Blackie." She burst into tears.

Lara glanced ahead. "We're all right while there's plenty of traffic. He can't pass us. How far to go?" She said it loud enough for Emily's father to hear. He replied, "A mile, I'd say. We passed a big sign

157

just now. Can't say I'll be sorry . . . Oh no, now what's going on.

The traffic began to slow. The radio message had been effective. Within minutes the wildlife park's security forces had closed in on the entrance to Longleat, checking every car slowly through, looking for the station wagon, not really believing the message they had received: a gang of children in a station wagon with the escaped panther in the back!

The steady stream of traffic through the gates slowed to a crawl and a quarter of a mile back down the approach road the cars buffered to a halt; half a mile . . . three quarters, until the station wagon, too, began to slow.

It rounded a gentle bend, and far back down the road behind them the children heard the sound of a siren. They turned to see the flashing blue light of an approaching police car.

The traffic squeezed over to let it by. Even so it could only gain on them gradually. The road was hemmed in by tall birches in a wide expanse of woodland. The trees hugged the road on either side, leaving only a thin grass verge for the cars to mount.

"We've got to get out of here," hissed Lara. "We're trapped if we don't."

Jamie threw up his arms, gesturing angrily in both directions. "And where are we supposed to go, huh? We've had it." He looked at Ellen sobbing bitterly in the panther's fur.

In the front of the car Emily's father heard Ellen

crying. "What on earth is the matter with that child now? This is a nightmare."

Emily whispered to the others, "If we can't go that way or that . . . she pointed up and down the road, "Then we'd better go that way." She pointed through the trees, into the bracken and brambles. "We have to get out. It's the only chance."

She called to her father. "I think Ellen's being sick. You'd better pull over."

Her father hesitated. In the mirror he saw Emily look down at the small girl. "Urgh, yes. She is! Quick!" she lied.

In a panic her father swung the car into the verge and squealed to a halt. The Landrover, travelling too close behind, was taken completely unawares. Dan hauled the wheel wildly to the right and the vehicle lurched over the road's centre line.

"Look out!" yelled Sean.

There was a sound of tortured metal as the vehicle careered into the path of an approaching car, ripping along its side.

Even before the station wagon had stopped Jamie was out the door with Feather at his heels. In both directions the traffic had stopped. Horns sounded. The marksmen struggled to free his door from the twisted metal of the car he'd hit. He gave up and yelled at Sean to move aside.

Emily's parents sat in bewildered confusion as drivers swore and shook their fists. They watched as first Jamie, then Harry and Lara, raced round to the car's tailgate, wrenching it open. Emily slid out first.

"Come on, Ellen!" she yelled, dragging the smaller girl after her.

As Ellen jumped tear-stained and sniffing from the car, Blackie stood up to follow. The blanket slid from her flanks and she stood framed majestically in the open back of the car, surveying the chaos. All around the cars grew silent as passengers gaped in disbelief.

In the Landrover the marksman roared at his companion. "Get out, you fool! I can't move; get out!"

"The p-p-panther . . . " pleaded Sean as he was shoved resisting through the yielding door. Dan grabbed for his weapons as he slid across the seats, following Sean.

Jamie shoved Emily forward, pushing Ellen's hand into hers. "Run!" he screamed. "Now. I'll stop him!" He pushed Harry and Lara after them and gave the panther a heavy slap across its rump. It spun round, spitting. Its ears were flat and its raised paw was armed with hooked claws.

Jamie paled for a moment before the panther shrank back, turned and fled with the children. With a yowl of fury Scab leapt from the back of the station wagon and sped after them.

As they raced through the trees Jamie turned back to the Landrover. Sean had fallen out of the door and lay in a heap on the ground. Feather stood over him, teeth bared, threats boiling in his throat.

Dan was pulling his weapons out of the vehicle. Jamie leapt on him. "You don't need them," he shouted. "She won't hurt. She won't —"

Dan was a big man; he shoved Jamie aside easily. "Oh no; it nearly had you just then, didn't it?"

"She's frightened, that's all. Just let me . . ."

As he stood up the marksman shoved him down again. "Stay there," he ordered. "You've done enough harm already." He raced into the undergrowth, following the path the children had taken.

Jamie hardly noticed Sean. He leapt to his feet, calling Feather after him, and shot after the marksman. Without Feather standing over him Sean staggered to his feet.

The children blundered deeper and deeper into the wood. They were scratched by brambles and stung by nettles. They never noticed the red wheals, nor the trickles of blood as they charged on, gasping for breath. Ellen was dragged between Lara and Emily, her feet barely touching the ground, her breath a harsh scrape in her throat. By contrast Blackie and Scab kept up an easy rhythm, ducking under branches, leaping dead trunks. Harry brought up the rear, snatching glances behind him, the breath rattling in his throat.

The undergrowth thinned. They ran on, Ellen's eyes rolling in her head as she fought to suck a little breath through her aching throat. Emily snatched a glance at her as they ran. "She can't keep it up. She's had it."

"She must," Lara's voice croaked dryly. "Blackie won't go without her. She's got to keep going."

They broke free of the ground cover that fouled

their legs, staggering on to a narrow track. Emily stumbled to a halt, the breath grating in her throat as she gasped, "Got idea . . . quick. Blackie . . . Blackie, come . . . come here.

The big cat stopped, realizing the others were no longer up with her. Scab stopped, too. Together they padded back. With an effort Emily lifted the collapsing child round the waist. "Help me . . .' she gasped. They lifted Ellen's legs until she straddled Blackie's back and lay sprawled and wheezing. The big cat twisted its head to nose at Ellen's hair. Emily took the girl's arms and joined them under Blackie's throat.

Harry stood doubled over, hands on knees, sucking great gobs of air in long, rasping breaths into his lungs. "You've got to keep going," he coughed. "I can hear a motor . . ."

"Can't be . . . " said Lara wiping her hair out of her eyes. "The road's blocked. Remember?"

Harry straightened up, trying to hold back his aching breath while he listened. Emily was urging Ellen to hold on. "Just grip her fur tight. We'll hold you from the sides. She pressed the girl's arm. We'll be all right; you see."

Suddenly Harry's voice croaked urgently, "It's not coming from the road. It's close. It's somewhere near —" And his voice was drowned by the noise of a jeep as it rounded a bend in the narrow track, wheels ploughing through the bordering undergrowth. In it were four men: a driver, two in police uniform, one in game warden's khaki. All three passengers were armed with rifles.

The girls and the panther fled down the track. Their hearts pumped speed into their legs, and fear sucked more effort from their lungs as they struggled to keep abreast of the panther's smooth flow. Both girls held Ellen in place on Blackie's back. Scab sprinted behind, tail up, ears back.

Harry hadn't moved. He screamed after them, "Get off the track. They can't catch you in the trees. Get off . . ."

The girls heard his voice and looked back. Harry was waving his arms, urging them into the woods. Behind him the jeep loomed large as he stood in its path. A horn sounded and they saw the driver yelling to Harry to move aside.

The last thing they saw as they leapt into the wooded undergrowth was Harry turning to face the speeding jeep. As the driver braked, struggling to avoid Harry, the wheels locked and the heavy jeep skidded sideways and toppled over.

Lara saw her brother's arms go up to shield himself, but the brambles closed around them as they ran. "Harry!" she screamed, and the pain in her throat and chest, the fear and the threat all burst out of her in a bubbling flood of tears as she ran.

"Oh Harry: Harry!" she wept, the tears mixing on her streaked face with bracken dust and bloody trickles.

On the path behind them, following their blundering tracks with ease, appeared Dan. He stopped, looking along the path for a moment to where the jeep lay on its side, a wheel still turning. The men were picking themselves up. One was kneeling beside Harry.

Dan hesitated, turned his eyes to the ground, and at an easy run followed the girls and the panther. A short way along he reached the point where they turned off the track. He turned off after them.

The girls ran blindly on, the agony of each breath lancing at their lungs. Ellen lost her hold and slid sideways. They pulled her upright on the panther's back. Blackie's progress had slowed with the extra weight; somehow she understood the need to have the girls at her side. Scab ran relentlessly behind them, sometimes jumping, sometimes slinking low under the ground cover.

A voice cut in on their rasping breath and their aching thoughts; a tinny sound, electronic; a voice through a loudhailer, calling instructions. "This is the police. Children, this is the police. The panther is dangerous. It is dangerous. Keep away from the panther. Don't be afraid. We are armed. You will not be hurt. Keep away from the panther. It is dangerous . . . "

The voice continued, repeating its warnings. It was directly ahead of them, and close.

Emily shook her head with desperate rage. "The fools," she gasped. "Why don't they understand."

She pushed Blackie's head round, away from the noise. They were stumbling now, relying more and more on their grasp on Ellen and Blackie to hold them up.

"Go – go on," she urged Lara. "Keep going . . . I'll try and lead them away."

Lara nodded, stumbling on with Blackie and Ellen, no breath left to answer. Emily stood, knees wobbling, acid bile searing the sides of her throat. The loudhailer was closer. She stood bowed, her chest heaving for breath, waiting. She wiped her face on her arm and raised her head. Her eyes were wet with sweat and tears, sticking her lashes together. They saw her before she saw them.

"There's one!" She heard a voice call. She saw a head in a blue cap above the chest-high undergrowth. And another; and another.

"If they can only see my head," she thought, "they won't know Blackie's not with me." She turned and stumbled away in a different direction. She heard a voice call for her to stop, and ignored it. She glanced up; there was another face, showing a khaki tunic at the shoulders. It was the man who had been driving with Sean.

And further over was the jeep. They were all round her. The only escape was the way Blackie had run. There was no choice but to follow. She forced herself after them, choking and spluttering as tears flooded her eyes and nose and throat.

A thick root snatched at her foot, and her tortured leg muscles collapsed, sending her skidding to the ground. She lay still for a moment, gasping the dusty air, before crawling on her stomach and elbows under the shelter of a stand of bracken.

As she lay in the dust, biting back the noise of her rasping breath, she heard the approach of feet through the ground cover. They were close. Through the maze of bracken stems she saw a pair of thick, heavy boots stride into view. They paused and went on, following the direction the panther had taken. They were followed by another, smaller pair, this time in sneakers. Somehow Sean had overtaken Jamie and was close behind Dan.

A surge of pain lanced between Lara's ribs with every stumbling step; her cheeks were hollow and dry, and her ears burst with the sound of pumping veins drumming at her temples. There was nothing left inside to feed her will. She wept tears of pain and frustration which blurred her vision as they floated dust and grime down her face and neck.

"Can't . . . can't hold you," she blurted to Ellen. The young girl lifted herself up on her elbows where she lay on Blackie's sleek back, oiled now with sweat. Ellen had recovered a little. The headlong dash that had destroyed the others had given her a little time to regain some breath. "I'm all right,' she urged. "I can hold on. Don't stop. It's getting easier."

She was right. The brambles thinned under the broad spread of the slim-trunked trees. Lara wiped the sweat and tears from her eyes, blinking. Ahead of her she could see a swathe of grass with coppices scattered over it like islands. In the distance she could make out a group of animals, moving slowly across the open ground.

They were giraffes. Giraffes, peacefully wandering through the English countryside. The absurdity might have made her laugh, had she any strength left with which to laugh. Instead she pointed, croaking to Ellen. "It's Longleat. We've made it. Keep going. Keep – uh!"

Her foot disappeared into an ancient ditch, hidden beneath the bracken, and three-quarters filled with leaves. As Blackie and Scab sensed its presence and cleared it with ease, Lara's body slammed to the ground. She wheezed harshly as her winded lungs fought for air; but Blackie and Scab kept relentlessly on. Ellen seemed unaware that Lara had gone. She, too, had seen the giraffes and the open ground, and the possibility of escape beckoning like a dream.

She bounced like a sack on Blackie's back. "We're nearly there," she whispered. "You're going to be all right."

Then she saw the fence. Her face froze as she traced its length, spreading like a silver ribbon in both directions as far as she could see, and inside it another. Two chain link barriers reaching metres high above her, with a three-metre no-man's land between; and at their tops, barbed wire strands that curved over on the grounds within.

Ellen's mouth was fixed open in dumb horror. "Stupid, she thought; of course there would be fences. How could they have been so stupid?"

Thirteen

Blackie reached the fence and slowed with Scab beside her. Ellen looked around, fingers gripping hard into the fur with desperation. She urged the cat forward along the boundary, not really knowing why, but to give up now was unthinkable. Maybe there was a hole.

They loped on. The ground had been cleared to make room for the fence, and here and there cut trees lay at crazy angles against their fellows, where they had been arrested in their fall.

Ellen heard voices. She hauled Blackie to a halt, listening. They were distant, ahead of her. Another, the loudhailer, sounded behind her. She chewed at her lower lip and her hands screwed nervously into the panther's coat.

She slid down from the animal's back. Blackie nosed into her face, whiskers trembling against the girl's cheek, while Scab flopped, panting, at the big cat's feet, his torn ear flicking.

Ellen sniffed back her fear. She pulled at the chain link, as if some divine influence might loosen it for her. It remained rooted firmly in the ground. A whimper escaped from her throat and the cats turned their heads to watch her. The voices were closer. She kicked at the links, peering up at the high top. Her eyes caught the tree branches and travelled along them and down the narrow trunks. Maybe over . . .

"Blackie . . . this way, Blackie," she called soothingly. The panther padded over to her and she coaxed it to the base of one of the half-fallen trees. "Go on." She pushed at the animal. Blackie rubbed her head against the girl, nearly knocking her down. Ellen stumbled backwards. "Go on!" she shouted. "You've got to or they'll shoot you." Her bottom lip wobbled, she opened her mouth to speak, and her face collapsed as the tears flooded through.

"Please go," she wept.

The big cat put its head down and nosed at Scab. Through her tears Ellen watched, remembering how the panther would not leave the shed without Scab. Despite Scab's growl of protest the small girl wrapped her arms round the tabby and picked him up. She plonked him on the angled tree trunk.

Blackie turned and placed her forepaws on the trunk, nuzzling Scab. Ellen was dwarfed by the stretched length of the animal. She bent down and tried to prise a black back paw from the ground and place it, too, on the trunk. The panther stepped aside and gently eased its front feet to the ground again. Scab jumped down, too.

"You must," blurted Ellen through the tears. Desperation overwhelmed her. "Go away!" she yelled. "You've got to go away." Her tears dripped

170

to the ground as she bent to pick up a short length of branch. She threw it. Blackie's ears went back as it whistled over her head.

At the edge of the undergrowth a figure stepped into view. The marksman watched the distraught child pick up another stick. He could hear her deep sobbing, and her yell, "Run away. Please, Blackie. I'm sorry . . ."

She raised her arm and hurled the stick. It hit Blackie in the side, and the panther cringed back, mouth wide in a noiseless snarl, uncomprehending and fearful.

The gunshot rent the air; unseen woodland creatures clattered through the trees and Ellen's whole body jerked with the shock. Blackie and Scab, too, leapt at the noise. Their eyes travelled to where Dan stood. His smoking rifle was pointing skyward. In the other hand he held a radio handset.

"It's got the girl," he said into it. "They're up against the fence, but I can't get a clear shot. I had to fire high to frighten it. It was going to attack. You'll have a better chance if you close in from the sides. But hurry."

Ellen couldn't hear the words. But she saw the man, and the smoking rifle. Fear for Blackie overcame her own fear. "Noooo!" she screamed as she rushed forward and flung her arms around the panther's neck. "Don't shoot! She won't hurt. Look, look. She's all right. We'll come. Don't shoot."

The nervous cat backed away with Ellen's arms round its neck, Scab spitting nervously at its feet, tail bushed. Ellen clung on. As the marksman watched in bewildered amazement Sean stepped out of the undergrowth behind him. He had come running when he heard the shot. "Did you get it?" he panted.

"What the hell are you doing here? I told you to stay back?" replied the marksman angrily.

His words were drowned by a crashing through the bushes as Jamie and Feather hurtled into view. Jamie, too, had heard the shot. He saw the rifle and flung himself bodily at the marksman. Feather buried his teeth into one thick boot. The man went down, handset and rifle spinning in different directions as he struggled to free himself from Jamie.

The rifle fell at Sean's feet. He looked to where the terrified girl clung to the panther. Jamie and the marksman still struggled on the ground. The panther was a big target, he thought, even with the kid hanging on to its neck. And he was a fair shot with an air rifle.

He picked up the rifle, sighted carefully along it, and squeezed the trigger. The explosion roared in his ears, filling his head with pain. The rifle recoiled and the stock kicked into Sean's nose. The boy was flung on his back through the brambles, blood flowing from his nostrils. The rifle dropped to the floor.

The shot hit a steel fence post centimetres above the big cat and whined away into the distance, leaving an angry gouge in the metal. Blackie screamed, in bewildered fear, hair stiff as black wire, the claws of one forepaw extended and ready to strike. Scab was beside her. The sudden reaction flung Ellen aside and she fell to the ground, terrified and weeping.

The shot separated Jamie from his adversary. He looked up and saw his sister lying still on the ground. "Oh my God!" he cried, as he leapt up and ran to her. Feather flew after him.

Other figures appeared in view in a wide, untidy semi-circle, a variety of weapons held ready: nets, sticks, guns. A voice ordered Jamie to keep away, but he ignored it.

There was a shout of "Jamie!" and Emily burst through the circle's edge on one side, followed by Lara. From the far side Harry leapt a fallen tree and barged through the brambles towards Ellen and the panther.

As they converged on Ellen, Emily panted, "They got past us. We had to wait for a chance to catch up."

Behind them a voice called. "Keep your guns up. They're too close." Dan had retrieved his rifle. He glanced angrily at Sean, who writhed, groaning, on the ground, his hands to his shattered nose.

Relief swept over Jamie as he ran to his sister and she climbed to her feet; but her sobs went on without break, a hopeless, helpless, hysterical, body-shaking wail.

She flung herself into him. "Oh Jamie," she sobbed. "You've got to save her. They'll shoot her. They're going to; I know."

"Shhh," he soothed, as the others ran up. "Maybe we can show them she won't hurt."

"You reckon?" said Emily. "I think they're too stupid to realize. Look how jumpy they've made her."

The panther was pacing back and forth against the fence, mouthing a snarl as she did so.

"They're getting closer," Lara called. "Spread out so they can't get a shot."

"I tried . . . I tried to make her jump over," Ellen gulped, indicating the fence. "But she wouldn't leave Scab."

The loudhailer sounded. "Children. You must lie down. Lie down now. So we can see the panther."

Jamie looked up at the fence, shaking his head. "That's too high," he said gently.

"She might've gone up that tree. But she wouldn't leave me. Me and Scab." Ellen buried her head in her brother's stomach and wept bitterly.

Emily studied the fence, and the fallen tree, thinking. She grabbed Jamie's arm. "Could you throw a rock over there?" She indicated the fences.

Jamie nodded. "Yes, but what —"

"What about something heavy; a log, say."

He nodded, bewildered.

Emily dodged round him to the two cats, pacing and prowling at the foot of the fence. The loudhailer once again ordered them to lie down. She scooped up Scab, who growled suspiciously, claws ready. Blackie's ears pricked and the yellow eyes watched intently as Scab was borne away. Emily ran back to Jamie, holding out the tabby.

"Throw him," she ordered. "Throw him over the fence."

Jamie's jaw dropped. "Pardon?"

"Do it!" she shouted. "There's no time for anything else. Maybe Blackie will follow."

"But there's barbed wire up there. He's not going to make it easy. I might kill him."

A sob choked out of Emily's throat and she gulped it back. "Huh; it'd take more than you to finish off this old ratbag. And anyway, cats always land on their feet." She held the tabby's coat briefly to her cheek and whispered, "Sorry,' in its half ear.

Purposefully Scab tried to claw free of her arms. She held him out to Jamie and smiled. "You'll do it," she said. "I know you will."

Jamie swallowed. "But Emily; I – I know what he means to you. I can't . . . "

She continued to hold out the struggling cat. "You must," she said softly, "There's no other way."

Jamie took the cat. It sank its teeth in his arms. Feather growled. The tabby coat puffed out in fury. Jamie winced as the claws scored a line down his arm. "I can't get a hold if it!"

Lara called. "Be quick. They're too close."

The men were confused. They couldn't shoot; the children were too close. They walked cautiously forward, guns ready for the worst.

"Run at them," yelled Emily, "Spoil their aim."

With the exception of Jamie, who was untangling Scab from his arm, they rushed at the armed men, waving and weaving left and right to confuse them. Jamie finally got a hold on the scruff of Scab's neck. The other hand curled under his belly. Blackie scowled at him, head bobbing and weaving to keep her eyes on the tabby.

Jamie swung Scab experimentally. The furious

cat screamed. It hooked with its back feet, tearing the flesh of Jamie's hand. The arc of swing widened. The cat's hair was electric with anger. Blackie roared in sympathy and moved forward, a paw raised. Jamie's arm rose to the peak of its swing and with a last grunted effort he flung his arm skyward, releasing his hold. The tabby ball spun flailing and howling through the air, turning over and over.

Blackie stopped, eyes tracking the object as it spun higher. She turned to follow it. The tabby cleared the first fence in an arc and began to drop. On the ground the children were closing on the marksmen, who watched in disbelief as Scab soared screaming over the high fence. Jamie held his bloody hand to his mouth as the cat dropped. It clipped the outer strand of barbed wire with a howl of rage and spun further out as it fell. It plummeted groundward writhing and twisting in the air, falling, falling until —

There was no dull smack as a broken carcase bounced on the earth; no squeal of pain. An angry cat, four feet spread, hair stiff as needles, stood slightly bewildered, looking round at its new view of the world. It shook each paw, peered back through the fence and spat angrily at Jamie.

"Wow!" whispered Jamie with huge admiration. "You really are some cat!"

Blackie was at Jamie's side, peering through the wire, running urgently from side to side, seeking a way to join the tabby. Scab had had enough. He raised his kinked tail and hurried at a dignified run through the tall grass towards a nearby coppice.

Blackie yowled in anguish, head searching for a way through. Jamie was beside the fallen tree, desperately calling her to it. The others had gone as close as they dared to the men and were running back, still keeping between them and the panther.

Blackie turned and stared stonily at Jamie. Her eyes ran along the line of the sloping trunk. She looked back at the disappearing figure of Scab. Suddenly she swung round and sprinted to Jamie and the tree.

"It's going for the boy," yelled one of the men, raising his gun as the big cat sprang. But Blackie cleared Jamie and hit the angled trunk, still running. Without breaking stride she flowed up the trunk and leapt lightly to a living tree high above. From there she stepped on to a high branch that stretched towards the fences. The branch bent under her weight. The children, standing tensely silent, watched in dread.

But Blackie never faltered. Trees were her home. The long-ago home in which she was born had been a deep, green place where her kind played high above the ground. She uncoiled her supple length and sprang, her tail rod-stiff and straight out behind. The whole group watched open-mouthed as the black shadow soared overhead.

It drifted over the fences, soft underbelly outlined against the sky, before it began to descend in a gentle arc that showed the sleek head and the muscled shoulders streamlined against the wind.

She flowed gracefully to the ground and her feet touched without a sound; and as she touched, her hindquarters gathered for her next stride. She sprang swiftly forward, following after Scab, whose tail had disappeared now, into the distant trees.

Outside the fence, a cheer went up from the five: Ellen wiped the tears from her grubby face with the bottom of her T-shirt, grinning up at her brother, hugging his arm; Harry and Lara flung their arms around one another and danced absurdly in the bracken; Emily smiled across at Jamie; and Jamie grinned back.

All around them stood men with guns and sticks, one carried a net; all their faces carried bewilderment, tempered with anger. They were beginning to feel they had been made fools of. Silently they looked from girl to boy.

Emily coughed. "I can, er . . .explain," she began. "But it might take a little while."

The five were slumped around the edges of the empty shed; empty but for a small pile of coins stacked in the middle of the floor. They studied it. There were no mice, no foxcubs, no birds. The only creatures were sounds, nibbling purposefully at a dandelion leaf, and Feather, flopped at Jamie's feet.

"Well, *I* don't think it's fair," said Ellen, folding her arms. "It wasn't *our* fault they were all stupid. And we didn't make that silly man crash his Landrover."

"Shut up," muttered Jamie.

"Yes, shut up."

Ellen flounced round on her bottom to face Emily. "You would agree with him, wouldn't you. Why aren't you my friend anymore?"

"I am, stupid; but I'm his too."

"Let's get on with it," said Lara.

Harry reached forward and picked up the coins, running them through his fingers. He handed them to Lara who counted them in five piles. "Ten each. Not much, at the end of it all."

"Just think what we'd have if Sean hadn't wrecked everything," sighed Emily.

Lara counted off on her fingers. "We wouldn't have had to pay for the wrecked car; or cleaning cat food out of your mum's station wagon; or replacing the mice . . ."

"I wonder how they got out," mused Harry.

Jamie shrugged. "Probably the neighbourhood kids. I bet they sneaked in while we were away."

"I still don't believe the grassnake ate them, though."

"Who, the kids?"

Jamie threw a lump of dried mud and it exploded with a puff of dust on the wall behind Harry's head. "No idiot, the mice."

Emily swivelled round so she was on her knees, optimistic as ever, "Let's look at the plus side: Rescued the crow, rescued the foxcubs. Dracula's back in the air, and the RSPCA will return the foxcubs to the wild as soon as they're old enough. We couldn't have kept an eye on everything forever. Not with school coming up. The hedgehog's always going to be hanging around. He was outside our door last night looking for food. We get free entry to Longleat for life, and our picture in the paper with the owner, Lord Bath . . ."

Ellen interrupted. "He was a very nice Lord,

wasn't he. I'm glad he's keeping Blackie." She paused, remembering the days when the neighbourhood children watched her with the panther in wide-eyed awe. "But it's not as nice as having her here all the time."

A long silence hung among them. Their eyes moved to Emily who was staring into the floor, lost in her thoughts. They know what she was thinking. Every day they found her somewhere, her eyes looking far away, to the day she first met Scab.

Jamie nudged her. "He'll be all right," he whispered gently.

She nodded sadly. "I suppose so. But I just wonder why no-one's seen him. I'm surprised he and Blackie didn't stick together. What if he's lying hurt somewhere? If only I knew he was okay."

"Lord Bath's game wardens are looking out for him," said Jamie. "They'll call us straight away if they see him. They promised."

Emily sighed. "At least Mum's stopped sneezing."

"And our dad took the mynah bird," said Lara, finishing off the list.

"It hasn't said anything for him yet," groaned Harry.

"Maybe he'll learn to love it before it does," soothed Emily.

Jamie studied her curiously. "Summer was looking boring until you turned up, then it got positively dangerous!"

She smiled at him. "Still, no bones broken, eh?"

"Sean; you forgot Sean," said Jamie.

Emily put her hand to her mouth. "Oh yes, how is he?"

"Well, his nose will never be the same again. Maybe that's a good thing. Every time he looks in a mirror it might remind him to be nice."

They laughed quietly, without malice.

Fourteen

The Landrover cruised to a halt, its engine running. The five children peered out through the closed windows. In the far distance a line of giraffes plodded in slow motion across the gentle English countryside; a pride of lions sunned themselves at the edge of a copse.

A big, ruddy-faced man peered out with them. "The wardens saw Blackie in this area yesterday. They were a long way off, but they're certain there was something with her; something small. They're not often wrong . . . " He paused. "But they could be. I'm afraid, children, you may have to face the fact that he's gone for good."

Lara put her hand on Emily's shoulder. "He could be right," she said gently. "I know it was all for the best, but being thrown over the fence like that . . . it could put you off the human race forever."

"If only we could get out and have a walk round and call for him," said Emily.

The ruddy-faced man spoke again, a sombre note in his voice. "I'm sorry, my dear; but we simply can't allow it. It would break every rule in the book. Even the game wardens don't wander far from their vehicles once they're in the wildlife park. Stay in the vehicle, keep the windows closed; that's the rule."

He sighed. "Please don't think me unsympathetic; but you must consider, too, what chance a tabby cat would have out here, among lions and monkeys; giraffes and rhinos . . . I'm afraid he might not have lasted very long."

Emily shook her head firmly, her mouth set, and turned to him. "You didn't know him," she said. "Honestly, sir, I know it's hard to believe, but Scab wasn't afraid of anything. The lion that tried to harm Scab would have scars to show it. We'll find him with Blackie. I'm sure of it."

"But my men . . ." began the head ranger.

"Scab wouldn't come out for them. He didn't trust anyone; only us."

"Only you," corrected Jamie.

"It's been two weeks," said Harry. "And we've been back and seen Blackie before. Why hasn't there been any sign of Scab?"

The head ranger signalled the driver to continue. The Landrover crunched into gear and drove on.

Emily returned her gaze to the rear window. "I don't know. Maybe Lara's right. How could he trust us after the way we treated him? Or maybe he hurt a leg when he landed. I know it didn't look like it, but who can tell? He did hit the wire."

"Maybe he's dead," said Ellen glumly.

There was silence in the Landrover as it bounced over the grass. They passed through a group of tall, ancient trees, their leaves yellowing in the autumn sun.

"Stop!" yelled Jamie. "She's there!"

The Landrover lurched as the driver hit the brake, sending them tumbling into a heap. Jamie hauled himself out of the head ranger's lap. "It's Blackie; in one of those trees."

Emily pressed her nose against the glass and peered up. The big cat blended into the high branch like an extra shadow with two yellow lights winking out of it. Emily quickly scanned the branch, and other branches; other trees. No sign of Scab.

It was no big surprise to find Blackie. As Harry had said, they had found her several times since she first leaped the wire into the wildlife park. She had settled down now. The publicity was over, and Lord Bath had agreed to keep her. Blackie seemed content in the quiet of the gentle Longleat plains. She had even padded over to the Landrover once or twice and stood while Ellen stroked her head through the open window.

It was Scab they were looking for. For two weeks the wardens had combed the open land and the wooded areas. They had left catfood – jellied sardines, his favourite – in the hope of tempting the tabby into the open. There had been not the slightest trace.

"If only I could get out," thought Emily. "If only . . ."

She looked round at the others. Everyone was straightening themselves out, dusting themselves down. She reached for the doorcatch. It clicked up and the door swung open, admitting a cool, clean breeze. She jumped down and ran clear of the Landrover.

"Emily!" came the sharp command of the head ranger. "Get back in the Landrover. Now! I insist!"

The warden had jumped from the driver's seat, rifle in hand, and was hurrying towards her.

"Sca-ab!" she called urgently. "Sca-ab; Scabby, Sca-ab. Oh, please come out. Please . . . where are you?" A single tear swelled in the rim of her eye, tumbled over the edge and coursed down her cheek. She felt the warden's hand on her arm.

"Better get back in, love. Sorry."

She sniffed back her tears, nodded miserably and allowed herself to be led back. She was climbing in when Ellen screamed. "Aaagh! I saw him. I did! Up there on the next branch. Above Blackie. See; where it splits into two."

Everyone looked. The warden forgot Emily as he peered, squinting, into the shrouded underside of the leaf canopy. Emily stepped clear of the Landrover for a better view.

Blackie was elegantly draped along a thick branch high in the tree. She peered down at them, unmoving. Occasionally an ear flicked. Above her the branches carried only the rustle of breeze-blown leaves.

"Sca-ab," called Emily again gently.

Nothing.

"He was there. Really; honestly. Oh, please come out, Scab," urged Ellen from the rear of the Landrover.

"Sca-ab," called Emily.

A head appeared on the branch directly above the panther; a tabby head with one ear split into little peaks, the other half-missing, and a scar that tracked across the pink nose and disappeared into the fur. It opened its jaws and mouthed a jagged scowl.

A cheer rose from the onlookers. The warden grinned happily, and even the head ranger raised his arms in the air and yelled, "Hurrah!"

Tears coursed down Emily's face, but she didn't care. She wiped her nose on her arm and whispered, "Scab; oh, Scab."

The stony face peered back; not a muscle moved.

"Shhh!" ordered Jamie. "Let Emily try. She's the only one who can do anything with him."

Emily called gently as she craned her neck up into the tree, peering at Scab.

His head retracted out of sight. An audible sigh sounded from the Landrover as everybody released their held breath in disappointment. Emily held up a hand. "Stay quiet. It's all right. It's just like when we first met. He's coming down; I bet."

"How do you know?" asked Harry.

"I just do. Wait."

Jamie pointed to the tree. "How's he going to get down. It's huge; and there's no branches for miles."

"He got up, didn't he? You'll see . . . look!"

Scab had appeared again. This time he was among the lower branches, where they sprouted from the trunk. Emily's heart thumped. "Don't frighten him," she told herself. "Take it gently; let him come."

She called his name; made her kissing noises between pursed lips. The tabby stretched its front legs down the perendicular trunk, testing the distance, feeling for a hold on the rough bark. In the Landrover they held their breath.

The cat paused, held back, and finally launched itself beyond the point of no return. It scrabbled and scratched, tearing deep gouges as it dropped and fell down the trunk. A slight lean in the tree had given him purchase; but the last four metres fell vertically. Scab struck a knobby growth and sailed into the air. With a scream of rage he twisted his body, spreading his four legs, bushing his tail, as he hurtled to the ground.

For the second time they watched him hit the grass soundlessly. Again he flicked each paw delicately; but he didn't walk away as he had done when Jamie threw him over the wire. He sat on the spot, wetted a paw, and used it to clean behind his ragged ear.

Emily watched him tenderly for a moment. "You great ugly brute," she whispered. She took a step towards him.

Overhead she heard a movement. She looked up to see the shadow-dark form of the panther launch itself from the branch high above. Blackie glided silently from the tree, far out over Emily's head in a graceful arc, flowing like water out of the air. She poured groundward in a rippling cascade that left them all spellbound, watching as she gathered herself to meet the grass.

She struck without a sound; a silent waterfall of fur, spilling to the earth and rearing skyward again as she hit; coming gently to rest beyond the Landrover, Emily and Scab.

As the momentum went out of her body Blackie turned. She slowed and stopped, her slitted eyes surveying them all. She mouthed her familar soundless miaow, so much like a threat. Emily looked at the panther, and at Scab sitting half-way between them. He was still washing himself with a studied lack of interest. The scarred tabby turned his head and peered long and hard at Blackie; then he stood, and padded slowly towards her.

"Call him," urged Lara breathlessly. "Call him, Emily, before it's too late."

Emily shook her head. "No. If this is where he wants to be, that's fine with me. I just wanted to know he was all right. I don't mind if he stays."

Scab stopped. He looked back at Emily. She felt his green eyes burning deep into her memory. Their brightness and depth mesmerized her; she knew she would never forget them.

They studied each other for long moments before Emily put her fingers to her lips, and blew him a kiss. "Goodbye," she whispered. "Good luck."

She turned and climbed into the back of the Landrover, hiding her crumpling face. Scab's head turned back to the panther. His kinked tail swished irritably at the grass. He looked again to Emily's disappearing figure, and took two steps towards it.

Jamie was rigid with excitement. "He's coming! Go on; call him. He doesn't know what to do."

"No." She nudged him softly, sadly. "You haven't

learned much, have you, you clot? That's Scab. You can't *make* him. He'll do whatever he wants."

The warden made to close the door. As it swung shut Scab's head rose further out of the grass, alert and interested. His ragged ear-and-a-half jerked forward and he moved swiftly towards them a few paces.

"Wait!" called Harry. He stopped the closing door. Scab turned and looked long and hard back at Blackie. The pair stood facing each other across the whispering, waving grass for long seconds, tail tips flicking. Finally, with a grumbling scowl the tabby rose up over the grass stems in a series of little leaps that took him closer and closer to the Landrover. With a final bound he cleared the rear door step and was in among them, purring and rubbing as they clamoured round.

Emily swept him from the floor. She held the warm, hard-muscled, purring body close against her chest, rubbing her cheek into the scarred head, matting the fur with her tears.

The warden gently closed the rear door, walked to the driver's seat and climbed in. The Landrover coughed into life and lurched away.

Ellen was at the back window, staring out at the diminishing figure of Blackie. "I still wish we could take her home," she murmured.

She was sitting on the head ranger's knee. "Never mind," he said. "We'll look after her, and you can all come and see her whenever you like. Tickets for life; you've earned them, all of you."

They watched through the rear window as the

black shape of the panther receded on the wide plain. They saw her turn away and pad lazily through the grass until she was hidden from view by a shallow rise in the ground. The Landrover cruised down the slope, heading for the gate.

Colin Pearce has written two other stories
about the adventures of Emily, Lara, Jamie, Harry
and Ellen. Make sure you read them both!

Something Really Terrible

The five friends secretly rescue a goat from its cruel
owner, the Weasel. But he finds out about it and
now he wants revenge. In his twisted mind that
could mean anything . . .

Something Really Dangerous

While messing about in the wilderness that passes
for their garden, the children find buried treasure.
They're convinced there's a whole hoard, and start
to dig in earnest. But there's more than just treasure
buried there . . .

And don't miss *The One Minute Dream*, a tense and
gripping story of a young girl's dream to skate the
length of her local esplanade in under one minute.

Something Really Terrible   £2.99 ❑
Something Really Dangerous   £2.99 ❑
The One Minute Dream   £2.25 ❑

All these books are available at your local bookshop or newsagent, or can be ordered from the publisher. To order direct from the publishers just tick the title you want and fill in the form below:

Name _____

Address _____

_____

Send to: Collins Childrens Cash Sales
　　　　　PO Box 11
　　　　　Falmouth
　　　　　Cornwall
　　　　　TR10 9EN

Please enclose a cheque or postal order or debit my Visa/ Access –

　Credit card no:

　Expiry date:

　Signature:

– to the value of the cover price plus:

UK: 80p for the first book and 20p per copy for each additional book ordered to a maximum charge of £2.00.

BFPO: 80p for the first book and 20p per copy for each additional book.

Overseas and Eire: £1.50 for the first book, £1.00 for the second book. Thereafter 30p per book.

ARMADA